Reginald Hill is a native of Cumbria and a former resident of Yorkshire, the setting for his outstanding crime novels featuring Dalziel and Pascoe, 'the best detective duo on the scene bar none' *(Daily Telegraph)*. His writing career began with the publication of *A Clubbable Woman* (1970), which introduced Chief Superintendent Andy Dalziel and DS Peter Pascoe. Their subsequent appearances, together with the adventures of Luton lathe operator turned PI Joe Sixsmith, have confirmed Hill's 'strong claim as our finest living crime writer' *(Sunday Telegraph)* and won numerous awards, including the Crime Writers' Association Cartier Diamond Dagger for his lifetime contribution to the genre.

The Dalziel and Pascoe novels have now been adapted into a successful BBC television series.

THE TURNING OF THE TIDE

The threat her husband had calmly issued when Emily told him she was leaving seemed extreme, even for the enigmatic, controlling Sterne Follet. Thinking about it now, as she languished in the sleepy, coastal town, Emily decided it was almost laughable. But her illusion of safety is abruptly shattered as a sequence of sinister events unfolds — culminating in the discovery of a body lying in the water's shallows. Now, Emily has the chilling feeling she is somehow involved in whatever is going on. So is her husband. But not necessarily on the same side . . .

Books by Reginald Hill
Published by The House of Ulverscroft:

TRAITOR'S BLOOD
NO MAN'S LAND
THE COLLABORATORS
MATLOCK'S SYSTEM
THE LOW ROAD
FELL OF DARK

JOE SIXSMITH SERIES:
BLOOD SYMPATHY
BORN GUILTY
KILLING THE LAWYERS
SINGING THE SADNESS

DALZIEL AND PASCOE SERIES:
DEADHEADS
EXIT LINES
CHILD'S PLAY
BONES AND SILENCE
ONE SMALL STEP
RECALLED TO LIFE
PICTURES OF PERFECTION
THE WOOD BEYOND
ASKING FOR THE MOON
A CLUBBABLE WOMAN
AN ADVANCEMENT OF LEARNING
AN APRIL SHROUD
ON BEULAH HEIGHT
RULING PASSION
ARMS AND THE WOMEN

REGINALD HILL

◆

THE TURNING OF THE TIDE

Complete and Unabridged

CHARNWOOD
Leicester

First published in 1971 under the title
'The Castle of the Demon'
and pseudonym of Patrick Ruell

First Charnwood Edition
published 2001
by arrangement with
Severn House Publishers Limited
Surrey

The moral right of the author has been asserted

British Library CIP Data

Hill, Reginald, *1936* –
    The turning of the tide.—Large print ed.—
Charnwood library series
1. Suspense fiction 2. Large type books
I. Title II. Ruell, Patrick, *1936* –.
Castle of the demon
823.9'14 [F]

ISBN 0–7089–9286–2

Published by
F. A. Thorpe (Publishing)
Anstey, Leicestershire

Set by Words & Graphics Ltd.
Anstey, Leicestershire
Printed and bound in Great Britain by
T. J. International Ltd., Padstow, Cornwall

This book is printed on acid-free paper

For Jean and Leslie

1

It had been a stupid thing to do, the quarry decided, crouching in the shadow on the deep side of the groyne.

He should have waited. He didn't believe in this need for desperate haste.

Not, of course, that it would be accounted 'desperate' by those who instigated it. Just a necessary acceleration of tempo.

'They' weren't crouched in this hollow, stinking of rotten seaweed, straining hearing through the low sullen roar of the sea and the beat of the racing heart for the sounds which would warn of pursuit.

Nothing.

Time to move.

He flipped easily, quickly, over the groyne, grunting as the ground met him earlier than he expected.

Still no sound behind. Perhaps he had made it. But it was too early to escape.

God! how his heart was going.

The pursuer, two groynes further up-tide, had seen the shadow flicker momentarily over the dimly silhouetted line. He nodded approvingly. A lesson well learnt. It was too early to close in. Or perhaps too late. He wished he knew which.

The quarter-moon was licked out of the sky by a tongue of black cloud.

Now he'd go. He rose slowly to follow. From

ahead came a clink of stone moved sharply against stone.

Careless. Very careless. Marks lost there.

Or perhaps marks gained. He might be very, very good, this fellow.

That should fetch him, thought the quarry. Now let's see if he's as good as he makes out. The thing is, he can afford not to be. You, he told himself contemptuously, you can be bloody brilliant and it matters not a toss. You're expendable. His heart felt as if it was trying to burrow its way out of his chest down into the sand beneath him.

He rose and moved in perfect silence to the next groyne. Over it in one silken movement. He didn't pause this time, but moved rapidly parallel to it down to the water. The last five or six yards, as the groyne buried itself in the sand, he slithered on his belly, pushing himself along with his elbows.

Try that for size, clever man.

From fifty yards out in the water the pursuer watched his quarry's entry with interest. He waited till he surfaced and began to swim steadily with the outgoing tide before making his presence known with a slap on the water.

Now let's see you *run*! he thought.

It was a test of speed now. The quarry swam well, his face buried deep in the water coming up for air on every fourth stroke, catching a brief glimpse of the little township which lay up against the seaside, one or two lights still twinkling, before it moved back into the darkness behind.

2

Twice he tried evasion. Once hanging on to a large piece of driftwood, the second time diving deep, deep. Staying there till his lungs threatened to burst and his crazy heart became erratic in its beat. Then he surfaced.

The pursuer was there, waiting for him. Never closing, always near.

So it was speed or nothing.

Was it worth it? Was it worth what? Anything. Anything. Would anyone even know?

His arms rose and fell like the flails of a paddleboat. He suddenly had a sense of not moving, of remaining constantly in the same place despite all his efforts. There was nothing to mark his progress against. He could see nothing of sky or shore. He shook his head violently to clear the salt water from his eyes but everything remained blurred. Only his heart was moving. It was rising up through his throat. It was swelling inside him. He felt its wild beating everywhere.

The pursuer saw his arms go up. Then he disappeared.

For a few moments the pursuer trod water, suspecting another attempt at evasion. Suddenly worried, he dived deep.

He had to dive three times before he found him.

Minutes later he dragged him up on a rock-strewn beach.

He was dead beyond the reach of any human kiss of life.

A pity.

There was little room on his clothing to carry

3

anything. A couple of pouches at his waist. Both empty.

He ran a knife down the skin-tight suit to facilitate taking it off. It unpeeled like the skin of a banana.

It contained nothing.

Nothing except the pale, fragile, curiously small body which lay at his feet on the sand.

For a moment he thought of taking the corpse back into the sea with him. Then he shrugged.

Why bother? The sea wouldn't want him. Better to leave him here where he would be found most like a man.

He rolled the mutilated suit up into a tight ball and fastened it by two loose straps to his wrist. It was a nuisance, but safer that way.

He turned to face the sea. It looked very uninviting. Suddenly he felt tired and cold. But walking back along the shore was out of the question, even along here.

He waded reluctantly out into the water and began to swim steadily against the outgoing tide. It was going to be a long haul.

And he was still not certain if he'd done a good night's work or not.

4

2

The sun had been perilously hot all day. For several hours, as though urged on by some primal sympathy, the sea had been edging its way towards the figure which lay burning on the sand, its only protection from the heat two scraps of flowered cloth. Once it had moved, turned floppily over on its back, arms slack, legs asprawl. But that had been two hours ago.

Now it lay quite quite still.

The sea was still twenty yards away, hardly clear of the smooth round stones which had scraped and rolled in the undertow for so long. Now they too were still and there was scarcely any forward ripple of waves. What movement there was no longer ran a new line of dampness along the sand. In a minute it would not even reach the full extent of the old line.

For a moment the water stood absolutely still. Nothing moved in sea, sky, or shore. Then the sea wrinkled its skin to shake off a puff of breeze.

It was not going to reach the figure. Not this time. There would be other times. It could wait. It shrugged a larger swell which broke in foam along the shore, and went into retreat. Immediately the breeze returned to the attack, grew into a wind, trailed an edge of grey cloud over the sun and ruffled the long yellow hair which lay like a sunburst round the figure's still head, bringing coldness where the sea had not been able to reach.

The girl opened her eyes and sat up.

The cloud blew by and she shielded her eyes from the sun as though staring out to sea. But her gaze was at first concerned only with herself. Expertly, appreciatively, she examined her body, noting the new patina of brownness the sun had burnt on her already deeply tanned skin. With her thumb she pulled back the bottom of her bikini and smiled at the radiant whiteness of the flesh revealed. It would have been nice if the deep golden-brown tan could have extended all over her body, but it didn't really matter. She didn't intend anyone see her with less covering than she had now. Not for a long time.

Still shading her eyes, she now gazed out over the visibly receding water. Lines of heat danced before her and the distance was becoming hazy, but the Scottish coast was clearly visible. Slowly she turned her gaze along from the distantly majestic cooling towers of Chapel Cross to the gentle swell of Criffel. Then jumping a dozen miles in a flicker of an eyelid she returned to her own side of the water. Here the only sign of human activity was a solitary fisherman by the water's edge far away to her left. Seated where she was she could see nothing of Skinburness village which lay even further in the same direction, while behind her rose the shelf of turf, gorse and bramble bushes which stretched back a hundred yards or more before it abutted on arable land.

Looking in this direction, she stood up. Now she could see at a distance of about half a mile the old house about which her childish imagination had created such fantasies when she first came here nearly twenty years earlier. Built of grey stone it stood solid and square to the shore, its straight lines broken only by the castellation of the roof parapet. It was only a hundred years old at the most she knew now. But between the ages of nine and thirteen for a fortnight each year it had served a variety of purposes, from an ogre's lair, via an English stronghold against the raiding Scots, to a kind of ultra-romantic Wuthering Heights. Then her mother had died and her father had never brought her here again. By the time she was thirteen she had known it was really a residential college belonging to Cumberland Education Authority. She supposed it still was.

Beyond it at a much greater distance back towards the village rose the cheerful red turrets of the Solway Towers, a solid-built hotel in Victorian Gothic. But her mind was not concerned with either of these buildings. Her sharp eyes were searching among the clumps of sea-grass for a familiar and distinctive shape.

'Cal!' she called, clearly but without stridency. 'Cal! Come on, boy! Where are you?'

There was no answering noise or movement.

'Cal!' she called again, more sharply this time. 'At once!'

But nothing stirred.

Puzzled, she began to follow her own tracks back through the sand towards the grass. Clearly marked also were innumerable and very large pawprints, but so confused that it was impossible to say whether they were coming or going. But after a few paces she halted and stared down at the sand, feeling vaguely uneasy.

Crossing the line of her own prints was another set, neither human nor canine. Wide, deep, beautifully defined hoof-marks. She followed them with her eye and found she turned through a hundred and eighty degrees.

Someone had ridden a horse down from the grass, circled her sleeping body on the sand at a distance of about fifteen yards, then passed on.

No, it hadn't been quite as simple as that, she decided, looking more closely. Here, at a point directly between where she had lain and the sea, the rider had paused. The horse had stood almost still, just shifting enough to interrupt the forward flow of the prints.

She shivered faintly at the thought of the eyes roaming freely over her unknowing body.

It's better than being spied on by some dirty old man lying in the grass, I suppose, she told herself, but instead of reassuring her, the thought only made her swing round to face inland.

Still nothing moved. She walked back to where she had been lying and gathered her possessions swiftly together. A pair of sunglasses and a white towelling beach-robe she had been using as a pillow. This she draped loosely over her shoulders and set off along the shore in the direction of the village.

Once she stopped, thinking she had noticed a movement in the grass to her left.

'Cal!' she shouted again.

The only reaction was from the fisherman who she noticed on resuming her walk had turned to look at her, attracted by her cry. On an impulse she turned from the line of the shore and moved diagonally across the sand and shingle (which intruded much further up the beach here) towards him. He watched her approach for a moment, then returned to the job of coiling his line at his feet, giving her a chance to study him at leisure. He was young, about thirty she guessed, well built, blond, wearing a broadly checked sports shirt and blue jeans tucked into rubber boots. He was coiling his line with a fluid economy of movement which was pleasing to watch, but he stopped when she was a couple of yards away and smiled at her with a disconcerting boldness.

'Excuse me,' she said, her voice pitched more coolly than she had intended. 'I've lost my dog. I wondered if you'd noticed him?'

'Dog?' he said, still smiling.

'He's rather large,' she said. 'You couldn't miss him. He's a kind of Old English Sheepdog.'

'Dog,' he said again, dropping the question mark and seemingly turning the word over in his mind as though trying to conjure up an image from it.

For a second she wondered if he was a foreigner, Scandinavian perhaps, having difficulty with the language. But now he laughed.

'Forgive me,' he said. 'I was just trying to picture what a *kind* of Old English Sheepdog looked like. But it doesn't matter, I'm afraid I haven't seen any kind of dog. I'm sorry.'

He studied her as if to gauge how serious a matter this was. He evidently decided it was not yet all that serious.

'In fact,' he added, kicking an empty fisherman's sack on the ground between them, 'I haven't seen any kind of livestock at all, flesh, fowl or good red herring. Especially not herring.'

He grinned again. It was a good grin, an honest, rather appealing English grin. She couldn't imagine how she had thought he might be foreign.

'You didn't see someone on a horse, then?' she asked, accepting his invitation to chat.

'On a horse?' he said.

Oh dear, she thought. Is he going to echo everything I say?

'No, I didn't,' he went on. 'Why? You haven't lost someone on a horse as well? You don't look the careless type.'

This time she joined in his amusement.

'No,' she said. 'It's just that I noticed some hoofprints on the sand back there where I was sunbathing.'

'Then there must have been a horse,' he said reasonably. 'It's just me. Once I set my mind to something, like fishing, for instance, I just don't notice anything else. You've been sunbathing over there, you say, and I didn't even notice you, which just goes to show!'

He looked her up and down admiringly.

'But I'm sorry I missed your dog,' he went on. 'Will he have gone far?'

'Oh no, I shouldn't think so. He usually doesn't stray very far from me at all. That's what makes it a bit funny. But I'll probably find him back at the cottage.'

'Cottage?' he said.

She didn't say anything but just looked at him. He looked puzzled, then flushed a little but grinned even more.

'Yes, it's terrible, isn't it?' he said. 'Everyone tells me I'm like an echo. It can be very irritating, I understand.'

'Yes, it can,' she said.

'But not to everyone. Some people like echoes. Anyway, this isn't finding your dog, is it? I'll walk back with you and put my mind to finding him. He doesn't stand a chance once I do that.'

Swiftly he bent and scooped up his line and bag.

'My name's Burgess,' he said, 'Arthur Burgess.'

'Salter,' she replied, with only the slightest hesitation. It would take a little time to get back into the habit of using her maiden name. But Sterne had been insistent on this point. 'Emily Salter. What are you laughing at?'

'You don't look like an Emily Salter, somehow. It sounds a bit maiden auntish and you certainly don't look like a maiden aunt. Sorry. I'm being rude, aren't I? Forgive me, Miss Emily. Let's look for your dog.'

Miss Emily. She glanced at her left hand and clenched her fist. The thin circlet of paler skin on her third finger stood out almost white against the even brown of the rest of her hand.

They walked along the shore in a silence which became almost companionable after a

11

couple of minutes. The sun was quite low now, shooting a line of varnished brightness up the Solway, laying a golden boundary between England and Scotland. The line of the tide running down to the Irish Sea was obscured by light. Her mind played with the phrase for a moment, then let it be washed away by the gentle lap of the ebbing water which, with their own footsteps, was the only sound. It seemed to merge with the silence rather than break it, just as the buildings that were now in sight seemed to lie flat against the frieze of grass, sea and sky rather than intrude into it.

'I'm at the hotel,' he said.

Hotel? she almost replied, but decided she didn't know him well enough. But already she recognised the tacit assumption somewhere deep in her mind that she would, and the recognition both surprised and worried her.

'I have taken a cottage,' she said. 'That one, there. The end of Long House.'

She pointed at the gable end of a rather ancient-looking building, set very low behind a broad sea-wall.

'By yourself?' he asked non-committally.

'No,' she replied. 'I'm with Cal.'

'Oh,' he said. No question mark this time, just disappointment.

'My dog,' she explained.

'Oh,' he said. 'Your dog. I see. That's nice. I'm at the hotel myself.'

'You told me.'

'No, I mean by myself. I mean, I'm not with anyone. Does that sound odd?'

12

'Why should it? Did I sound odd.'

'Of course not,' he said. 'I mean, you've got a dog. And a cottage. Why not? On the other hand, a lone man in a hotel. I have a table to myself and I dread to think what the others must think when they look at me at breakfast.'

'Why do it if it's going to worry you so much?' she asked.

'Why shouldn't I?' he said, a trifle aggressively.

She glanced at him and shrugged her shoulders. Perhaps she'd been wrong and wasn't going to know him better. She'd been wrong before.

'I'm sorry,' he said. Then he laughed with a slightly embarrassed note. 'There should have been a gang of us. A friend, a couple of girls. But it all fell through for some reason. So I came by myself.'

'I'm sorry,' she said.

'Now you're echoing me. Hey, does your dog resemble a sort of hairy patchwork pony? If he does, I think he's got home first.'

But Emily had already seen him ponderously detach himself from the still distant doorway of the cottage.

'Cal!' she called, running forward. 'Cal, boy!'

At the sound of her voice the huge dog's tentative steps turned into a majestic gallop and a bark deafening in its joyfulness broke the peace of the evening.

Burgess looked at the approaching shape and wisely decided to keep out of this welcome-home scene. Cal was indeed a kind of Old English Sheepdog, but somehow or other he had got the

13

legs and quarters of a Great Dane. He flung himself with all the vast muscular power at his disposal on top of Emily, who braced herself like one well practised in meeting such assaults.

'Oh, Cal,' she said. 'You silly, silly dog. Where have you been? What have you been up to?'

Cal's tongue slapped her cheek warmly, damply, and discarding the dignity befitting his size he ran round and round her in a kind of waltz-time, always keeping his head as close to Emily as possible while his hind-quarters were unceremoniously flung round at some considerable distance behind.

Finally Burgess judged it safe to approach. Cal stopped and looked at him enquiringly. The man stopped too, feeling it was not perhaps so safe, after all.

'Cal,' said Emily quietly. 'This is Mr. Burgess. He is a friend.'

She held out a hand to her companion, who took it gladly.

Cal resumed his caperings and Emily let go.

'What a beast!' said Burgess admiringly. 'No wonder he got himself lost. With all that hair hanging over his eyes, he must be half-blind!'

'He is,' said Emily quietly. 'In his left eye. He sees very poorly at a distance. That's why I shout so much.'

'I'm sorry,' said Burgess.

'So am I. It was silly of me to tell you. It puts you at fault when you're not really at all. Forgive me.'

They had begun to move forward again, Cal loping ahead, glancing back from time to time to

14

ensure he was followed.

'On condition,' said Burgess suddenly as they reached the track which turned away from the sea up towards the hotel.

'What on condition?'

'I'll forgive you on condition. On condition you come and have dinner with me tonight.'

'Up there, you mean?'

She made a motion of her head towards the red-tiled turrets. Her hair fell in a disturbingly beautiful sweep over her right cheek.

'Or anywhere else you want.'

She thought so long and so impassively it seemed certain she would refuse.

'All right,' she said finally. 'Up there. What time shall I come?'

'I'll collect you at seven,' he replied. 'If that's O.K.?'

'Fine,' she said. 'But don't call. I'll meet you there. It's only a short walk.'

She walked away to where the big dog stood impatiently waiting.

'All right,' he called after her. 'In the bar. Seven o'clock. Don't be late.'

'Late?' she said to him over her shoulder.

They both laughed and he stood watching her till she and the dog had disappeared into the cottage.

Now what did I want to go and do that for? she asked herself as she opened the cottage door and went inside.

A lone bachelor, let down by his girl friend. A casual pick-up on the beach. He'll probably start sending out feelers under the table between

15

the soup and the fish.

'What do you think?' she asked the dog, who had leapt tremendously on to a fortunately very solid-looking couch the moment he went in.

Cal hung his head over one arm of the couch and looked at her sagaciously and barked happily.

'Thanks,' she said, blinking against the gloom. More than gloom. It was downright dark, despite the bright evening sunshine which still covered everything outside.

It was called a cottage, but it wasn't one at all. 'Cottage' gave the impression of a small detached building with honeysuckle and roses climbing up the wall. This place was really a flat, if 'flat' didn't conjure up quite another and absurdly modern picture. It was the bottom floor of a two-storey semi-detached building. The whole building stretched in a terrace about fifty yards long (which was where it got its name Long House, she supposed), with wings at either end partially enclosing a cobbled yard. It contained half a dozen or more 'cottages' most of the front doors of which opened on to a sea-wall, with the hightide line not many yards away. Hers was the end one and the door opened to the side so that it faced up the long spit of land known as the Grune where she had been sun-bathing that day. But the bedroom windows overlooked the sea.

Windows were obviously a problem to the builders. The place was very old, how old she couldn't say. It had been built for solidity and contained none of the more commonplace evidences of 'style' which would have helped her to date it. Everyone said it was mentioned in Scott's *Redgauntlet* as some kind of hotel, and many of the cottage names were taken from the book. The Young Pretender was supposed to have slept there, and it may have been an old building then.

But, whenever it was built, windows had proved difficult. Or perhaps they had only become difficult later as domestic expectations grew higher. There were two bedrooms overlooking the sea, both well enough lit. The large one, hers, ran parallel to the living room and had two not very large but adequate windows. Similarly the other, smaller one. So they were fine.

The trouble was the living room. It shared one wall with the bedroom, one wall with the kitchen, a third (opposite the bedroom wall) with the cottage next door which formed the 'wing' of the whole of Long House; and thus the room only had one 'outside' wall. The front door was here, of course. But so was the fireplace, and this was huge.

The whole complex took up two-thirds of the wall. The door took up most of the rest. This left room for a window approximately two and a half feet square. Even with the help of a glass panel over the door this was totally inadequate to light what was a very long room.

So with a casual ingenuity which Emily greatly admired, the builder, or some later 'improver', had knocked a small window high in the wall between the bedroom and the living room so that the superfluity of light in the former could be democratically shared with the latter.

It worked reasonably well at midday in bright sunshine. At most other times the electric light was needed, despite an additional aid to the lighting problem in the form of a multiplicity of mirrors. They were everywhere in the lounge: square ones, round ones, long ones; fitted into furniture, nailed on to walls, resting casually on top of the sideboard. Her favourite was the one high above the double mantelshelf of the fireplace, too high to reflect herself unless she stood on tiptoe.

Perhaps the real reason she liked this mirror was just because she could not see into it. All the mirrors were pretty old, with some of the silvering going, and though only one was actually cracked, none of them gave what seemed to be a simple true reflection. There was always a slight twist somewhere, or a mistiness. It made her feel slightly uneasy to come face to face with herself as suddenly as she could do here. She had been here nearly a week. Surely that was long enough?

For me, perhaps, she thought gloomily. But Sterne had booked her into the cottage for a fortnight; and Sterne Follett expected thirty-six inches in his yard.

She dared not plumb too deeply into her hopes and fears. Somewhere, fathoms below, struggling all the time to reach the surface of her mind, was the certainty that Sterne would never let her go. But he had implied a bargain; that was why she was here. And he kept his word, didn't he? She had to stay.

But he used people as well. In the end it might

18

all be for nothing. Probably for nothing. Nothing.

Still, it wasn't too bad. Being here. Not too bad. Not while the sun shone. She too would make a bargain, a meteorological pact. God alone knew what her husband was up to and she had no desire to share the knowledge. So let the weather decide.

Once the weather broke, she promised herself, she would go.

'Where next, Cal?' she asked. The big dog opened its good eye, then went back to sleep. It loved to lie on the couch whenever it got the chance. But at night Emily stretched out a large rug in the covered archway outside the back door and he slept there. The nights had been so hot and muggy since they came that if he stayed inside he would start licking her face in the early hours till she awoke and let him out.

Emily glanced at her watch. There was time for a cup of tea before getting ready. She still took an absurd pleasure in catering for herself, even at this lowly level. She had been ashamed to find how inept she was in the kitchen when she first started to look after herself again. That had only been a fortnight ago. It seemed much longer. But now at least she knew exactly where everything was.

She opened the door of the large store cupboard in the living room and reached inside.

Her fingers closed over a packet of tea instead of the tea-caddy.

She lifted it out and looked at it thoughtfully. It was very right and proper that packets of tea should be on the same shelf as the caddy. She had decided on the arrangement herself. But there shouldn't have been one there.

She peered into the cupboard, went and switched the electric light on, peered in once more.

There the caddy was, looking perfectly ordinary, neatly situated on the shelf, no sign of disturbance.

She looked at the next shelf. Two bottles of instant coffee looking exactly the same. She knew one was half-empty, one unopened. It was impossible to tell which was which till you felt the weight. But she knew the unopened one was nearest the side of the cupboard. She picked up the other, unscrewed the lid. The circle of unblemished silver foil shone dully at her like a great, unseeing, cyclopean eye.

Now she went swiftly round the house. Nothing was missing, nothing of hers, anyway. But here and there she found other small signs of disturbance, unnoticeable unless you looked closely.

She looked very closely, seeking firm evidence that this was more than the neurotic nervousness of a woman living alone. Finally convinced, she lay down on her bed and lit a cigarette.

I suppose I should call the police, she thought. For what? A lot of questions, a lot of disbelief. Christ, I can hardly believe it myself! Why should they? I'd probably get some big fat bobby who'd think I was trying to get a bit of male attention. He might even try his hand. Better forget it. I don't want to end up resisting

20

an officer in the pursuit of his duty!

Laughing to herself, she leaned over and stubbed her cigarette out in the ashtray on the bedside table. Beside it lay a book, with a matchstick protruding from its pages as a bookmark. She glanced at her watch. A cup of tea no longer attracted, but she still had a quarter of an hour or more before she needed to change.

She leaned back and opened the book. It was a nineteenth-century history of the Solway and seemed to go with the cottage. She had found it by her pillow on arrival, opened at the chapter on the 'busy and important port of Silloth'. It was fascinating reading. She had known the area from childhood, though she had not been back here for fifteen years or more. And delving into a past where familiar old names loomed large gave her a sense of security, a feeling of belonging.

'Religious houses on the Solway Coast,' she read. She gave a sigh of satisfaction and settled back into her pillow. She wished that she hadn't made that silly arrangement to go out. She could always telephone the hotel. But that would be unfair. One thing she had learned from the last ten years was that everyone deserved a fair deal. Even Sterne honoured obligations in his own way.

So as long as she honoured hers within reason, life would go on, become bearable eventually.

'Besides, I'm tired of omelettes,' she said aloud.

She arrived at the Solway Towers dead on time, having deposited Cal and a small thigh-bone in the pretty little hotel garden. He tended to be a menace in crowded bars.

It was her first visit to the hotel since she arrived in Skinburness, and the last time she had been there was more than ten years earlier. Ten aeons in terms of experience.

Burgess rose from his seat and greeted her warmly, but at least half his attention was fixed on a small gathering further along the bar around a woman on a high stool who was crying, drinking and talking at the same time. From the surrounding group arose a constant ululation of consoling coos. It was the kind of grouping and 'natural' noise you might expect from a rather poor repertory company with lots of amateur extras. The woman herself was undoubtedly professional.

Everyone else in the room was observing the main action with undisguised interest.

'For Godsake!' cried the leading lady with a nasal American drawl. 'Why doesn't someone get out and *do* something instead of just farting around? He's lost, I tell you. He's in trouble! Won't you even phone the coastguard?'

This last question she snarled at a man who from the quality of his cooing and the nature of his dress Emily assumed was the manager.

'Please, Mrs. Castell,' he said. 'What I can I will do. But I do not see . . . your husband is merely forty-five minutes late . . . we will keep his dinner for him. Perhaps something of interest occupied his attention. There is no danger, I assure you. It is early yet . . . '

'Early!' cried the woman. 'Early! You want to

wait till it's late, is that it? And no danger? What about that guy they found drowned on the beach down the coast a ways only last week. Try telling him there was no danger, eh? This couldn't happen at a Hilton hotel.'

'What on earth is going on?' whispered Emily to Burgess.

'The lady,' he replied, 'is Mrs. Amanda Castell, whose husband, Mr. Fenimore Castell, set out for a preprandial walk about five o'clock from which he has not yet returned. She is convinced that he's fallen into a creek or trodden on quicksand. Mind you, it wouldn't have to be very quick. He is a very large man and even good firm earth yields to his tread. I think that's why they don't walk together. Double the danger.'

Satirical Mr. Burgess, thought Emily. But without doubt Mrs. Amanda Castell was a large woman. Twenty years earlier her figure might have been Junoesque.

Now the front curves had resolved themselves into a single mighty undulation.

But she had a pleasant, rather likable face and something like amusement glittered at the back of her eyes as she caught the tail-end of Emily's scrutiny.

'She's right, though,' Burgess went on. 'The water round here is dangerous. I hope you don't get your bathing suit wet when you're by yourself?'

'I'm careful,' she said, part amused, part irritated by his warning. 'It was sad about that chap they found. It was at Allonby, wasn't it? I read about it in the local paper the day I arrived.'

Allonby was about nine miles down the coast. She could remember going to have tea in a café when she was young, then playing among the rocks on the beach. It was a much-looked-forward-to treat. Her memory drift prevented her from catching the first part of her host's reply. She gathered he had been talking about the inquest.

' . . . heart-failure,' he said. 'He wasn't wearing a stitch, evidently. Perhaps the sea had dragged his clothing off him. Anyway, identification was impossible further than the fact that he was a foreigner. No one's come forward to claim him.'

'How'd they know he was a foreigner if there were no clothes?'

'Teeth,' he said laconically. 'They weren't filled by an English dentist.'

'Perhaps he fell off a boat,' suggested Emily, as the barman approached.

He looked pleased to have something to do other than minister to a grieving woman.

'Gin and tonic,' she said to Burgess's questioning eyebrows.

'And a half of keg,' he passed on to the barman.

'And a pint of Guinness when you've a moment, John,' said another voice.

It came from a man leaning through the hatch which opened from the bar on to the smoke room. Through it came the click of dominoes and the chatter of male conversation. The man was tall, in his thirties, with jet-black hair and a weather-beaten face of rather sullen cast.

'Right, Mr. Scott,' said the barman.

Scott's attention seemed like everybody else's to be on the American woman who had started talking again. The corners of his mouth lifted sardonically as he listened, then his gaze drifted momentarily along the bar, took in Emily and Burgess, held them for a moment, and returned to the main attraction.

Emily felt discarded, but reassured herself by basking in the full glow of Burgess's obvious pride of possession now he had returned his whole attention to her.

Even this was not hers for long, however. Behind her she heard the bar door open.

'Fenimore!' screamed Amanda Castell in a high C of relief.

Then 'Fenimore!' she added, dropping an octave into menace, 'where in the name of all that's holy have you been?'

If the man you're with is staring over your shoulder, Emily told herself resignedly, you might as well look with him. But before she did, she noticed with mild curiosity that the man Scott had decided to ignore this interesting development and had moved away from the hatch.

Fenimore Castell *was* large. He filled the doorway, just as honest distress at his wife's question filled his broad honest face which had a look of perpetual surprise given to it by a pair of huge rimless spectacles fastened round the back of his head by an elastic band.

'Honey, I'm sorry! Have you been worried? I never thought . . . the time just flew. The thing was this. I came across Mr. Inwit and Mr.

Plowman here — you remember we noticed them at dinner last night and you said — well, anyway, here they are.'

With the air of a jovial conjuror he shepherded forward two men who had entered almost unnoticed behind him.

Both middle-aged and of medium height, there the resemblance ended. The one on Castell's left was round, with a chubby red face in which bright little eyes twinkled behind thick-lensed spectacles. A few scant locks of fair hair had been laid carefully over his sunburnt pate whose bald eminence shone like polished red tiles.

The other was thin and lugubrious in appearance. His nose looked as if it had been pinched out of china clay and his thin lips pressed together in an unyielding line. He had all his lank brown hair and was wearing what looked like a boiler-suit, the knees of which were stained with fresh earth.

Oblivious to everyone else, Fenimore Castell was continuing his explanation to his wife.

'Now these two, Mr. Plowman and Mr. Inwit' (Which is which? wondered Emily), 'are archaeologists, honey, the real thing, yeah. And I found them at it along the Grune!'

A half-choked sound came from Burgess at this. He buried his face in his beer glass.

'It seems there used to be a chapel situated out there on the Grune . . . '

'What in God's name is this Grune you keep on talking about?' interjected Amanda.

'It is the name given,' said the thin

archaeologist drily, 'to the peninsula about one mile in length and one quarter-mile in width bounded by the Solway on one hand and Skinburness creek on the other which extends from Skinburness village to the headland or spit known as Grune Point. The etymology of the word has been open to some speculation in the past, but now it is generally agreed that it is a variant of 'groyne', whose modern sense is a manmade barrier against the erosion of coast-land by the sea.'

'Isn't he great?' Fenimore asked everybody with pride. 'Anyway, there they were in the middle of this patch of gorse and furze, digging away. I offered my assistance, as a common labourer merely, and I confess I lost all track of time.'

'You've been exerting yourself, blossom?' asked his wife, now all loving anxiety. 'And you with your heart condition? Come upstairs now and take one of your green tablets, and lie down for a while before dinner. Which we would appreciate *hot!*'

With this last shot at the management, she ushered her unprotesting husband out of the bar, her only acknowledgment of Inwit and Plowman being an indignant glare at them as she went through the door.

'Phew!' said Burgess. 'How's your drink? I too like my dinner hot.'

'Upon which hint . . . ' said Emily downing what remained of her gin. 'Come on, lead the way.'

It was a pleasant evening, spiced rather than spoiled by the unexpected incidents which surrounded it. They exchanged a little information about themselves, though Emily did not show much curiosity in case it was returned. Burgess, she discovered, was a personnel officer with some large concern in Manchester. She told him she was a secretary, which seemed anonymous enough till she caught him looking at her very expensive dress and accessories. To distract him, she told him about her suspicions that there had been someone in her cottage that day. He was concerned, which she had expected, but also questioned her very closely about matters of detail which had aroused her suspicions, which she found a little bit strange.

'What are you trying to prove?' she finally asked. 'That I'm just a nervous woman living on her own and imagining things?'

'I hope you are,' he said with a grin. 'But you don't seem very nervous to me. I'd say you were quite capable of looking after yourself.'

She was pleased when he did not attempt to contradict her decision not to call the police. But despite her protests he insisted on walking down from the hotel with her to the cottage.

'Don't forget Cal,' he said, as they came out of the hotel.

As if in answer, from the hotel garden there came a deep hoarse growling bark.

'Something's up,' said Emily. 'Come on.'

In the small garden an interesting tableau awaited them. Cal, his head cocked to give maximum scope to his good eye, was standing stiff-legged, growling more in wonder than in anger at a huge jet-black cat which crouched on the lawn before him. The cat's teeth were bared in a soundless snarl and its tail was lashing back and forward over the neatly mown turf.

Burgess laughed.

'You'd think he'd pick on someone his own size.'

'Careful,' said Emily, restraining him from moving forward. 'That brute could tear his other eye out before he got a grip of it.'

She bent, picked up a handful of gravel from the path and tossed it gently at the cat. The beast looked at her balefully for a second but didn't budge.

She picked up a second handful and took her arm back, meaning to put a little more force into it this time, but her wrist was gripped from behind with quiet strength. For a second she thought it was Burgess.

'If you must use animals for target practice, try that donkey there,' said a voice with no humour in it.

She turned to find herself looking at the man Scott she had noticed in the smoke room.

'Let go of me!' she said furiously.

'Certainly,' he replied quietly, releasing her.

'How dare you?' she began, but her indignation died at the cold anger she saw on his face. He stepped over to the two animals.

'Miranda,' he said.

The cat looked up, then leapt effortlessly into his arms.

He stroked it gently and it purred with a vibrant intensity Emily could almost feel in her spine.

'You really must be careful of the company you keep,' said Scott to his cat. Without another look at Emily, Burgess or the dog at his feet, he strode away over the lawn and passed out of sight through a gap in the hedge.

Her indignation rising again, Emily turned to Burgess whom she saw several yards away in the shadows leaning against the hotel wall.

'I'm one of Nature's cowards,' he said. 'I like girls who fight their own battles.'

'Thanks a lot,' she said ironically. 'Who was that awful man? Is he stopping at the hotel? I've a good mind to complain about him.'

One thing about being Sterne Follett's wife, she told herself. You didn't get treated like that. Or if you did, it was quickly and efficiently dealt with. Burgess merely seemed to find it amusing.

'No, he doesn't stay here,' he said in reply to her question. 'Though he seems to spend a lot of time in the back bar here. His name's Scott. I think he's something to do with that place there.'

He waved his hand vaguely in the direction of the college.

'The college?' said Emily. 'I hope he's got nothing to do with educating students.'

Still angry, she strode vigorously down the lane which led to the shore, with Cal and Burgess trailing behind. No one spoke till they reached the cottage. She stopped at the gate.

'I won't ask you in, if you don't mind,' she said, surprised to hear herself speaking so defensively.

'That's all right,' he said equably. 'I'll just hang on out here for a second till you're sure all's well within.'

'If you must,' she said with a shrug, but none the less had a good look around inside before reappearing at the door.

'Not a burglar in sight,' she said. 'Well, thanks for a very enjoyable evening.'

'Yes,' he said. 'Me too. Perhaps we'll bump into each other again before you go. Good night.'

Geared as she had been to resist any attempt to prolong the evening, Emily felt curiously let down by this suddenness of withdrawal.

'Good night,' she called after the rapidly vanishing figure. He lifted a hand in acknowledgment, then disappeared in the gloom.

Thinking back on the evening as she lay in bed, Emily wondered what had caused the apparent cooling off in Burgess's attitude to her. Or perhaps it was all in her own mind, based on the assumption of her own vulnerability and desirability which her life hitherto had given her. Odd, though.

She began to read in her book a description of the great tempest at the beginning of the fourteenth century which carried away the road to Skinburness and part of the town itself, and a little while later fell asleep with the sound of the sea in her ears.

★ ★ ★

At three o'clock in the morning Emily woke suddenly with a fearful sense of being watched.

She lay quite still for what seemed several minutes, not daring to do more than strain her half-opened eyes into the gloom around. The room was full of shifting shadow and light cast by the restless movement of the sea not many yards outside her window. A light breeze stirred the flimsy cotton curtain.

I can't lie like this for ever, she thought desperately.

And in the same moment she sat up and reached for the light cord above her head. For one terrifying moment she could not find it. Then it was in her hand and light — bright, unflickering, yellow light — filled the room.

It was, of course, quite empty.

True, the window was open, but it was far too small for anyone to enter through. But when the curtain blew again, laughing at her own fears she got up to close it.

Outside a nearly full moon shone down on a sea which looked as if it was made out of beaten silver. It was incredibly beautiful and she stood for a long while peering out at it along the silver path which stretched all the way across to Criffel and the thread of red lights seemingly suspended in air, which she knew marked the masts of the American naval base at Caerlaverock.

A gush of affection for the place rose in her heart and with it a sense of well-being, of safety, of belonging. She took a deep breath of the salty air, decided it would be criminal to shut this out, and turned back to bed.

And let the fresh sea air out of her lungs in a long wavering scream as she saw the face peering down at her through the internal window.

★ ★ ★

'How long was it before you left your bedroom, Mrs. Follett?' asked the police constable.

Emily was sitting with a blanket draped round her shoulders in the kitchen of the upstairs cottage. Cal lay at her feet, yawning. Clutching a teapot in the background was Mrs. Herbert, the old woman who lived there. She looked very anxious and Emily found herself smiling reassuringly at her, then remembering it should have been the other way around.

The interrogative twist of the constable's eyebrows reminded her too. He seemed a pleasant young man and had cycled well over a mile to get to the scene of the crime.

The phrase was Emily's, not his. He was still trying to establish the existence of the crime.

'A couple of minutes, I think. I don't know.'

'And the face was there all this time?'

'No. No. It disappeared as soon as I screamed. I mean it. He, whoever it was, must have been standing on the couch in the living room to peer through, and when I screamed he just stepped down.'

'So you got an impression of this face moving down from the window?'

'Yes. I suppose I did. I don't know. He must have done.'

The constable wrote in his notebook. It was

reassuring to see that he used a ball-point pen instead of the traditional tongue-licked stub of pencil. And that he wrote a rapid but neat shorthand.

'But when you got through into the living room there was no sign of him?'

'No.'

'How closely did you look?'

Emily made an indignant noise which turned bubbly in her teacup.

'Not very closely, I tell you! I ran like hell through the kitchen and out of the back door into the courtyard.'

'The back door. Why not the front? It was nearer.'

'Outside the front door there's nothing but sea and shore. I didn't fancy that one little bit. And outside the back door was Cal.'

She bent and stroked the dog. The constable's face relaxed into a grin.

'A nice bit of thinking that, in the circumstances.'

He stood up.

'I'll just take a look around downstairs.'

'Are you all right now, dear?' asked the old woman as soon as the policeman had gone.

'Yes, thank you very much,' Emily answered. 'It's been very kind of you and I mustn't keep you up any more.' She put her cup and saucer (Crown Derby — the best for the guest) down on the draining board. 'I'm sure it's all right for me to go downstairs now. I'll give you your blanket back in the morning if I may.'

She pulled it tightly around her. Even

policemen were human.

'There you are, Mrs. Follett,' he said, as she came into the living room. He was standing on the couch looking at the internal window. 'I think we can let you get back to bed now. If you'd just check there's nothing missing first.'

'What? Oh, of course.'

It took her only a couple of minutes to check.

'No, nothing. I mean certainly nothing of mine. And as far as I can see, nothing belonging to the cottage.'

'I see. Thank you very much. Well, I'll be on my way. Perhaps you could contact us in Silloth if anything else occurs to you which might be helpful. And we'll be in touch ourselves. You'll be all right now?'

'Of course,' she said. 'Cal's staying in with me. He'll just have to sweat a little. I've sweated enough tonight.'

'Better lock up after me, eh?' he said, leading the way down the corridor to the kitchen.

He paused at the door and asked casually, 'You had to unlock this to get out into the yard, did you?'

'Why yes. Of course.'

'Was the key in the lock?'

'Yes, it was. I think it's sort of welded in. But it was locked. *And* the bolts were in.'

Why do I sound so defensive? she wondered. He moved the upper bolt back and forward. It was rusty and very stiff. Emily held out her hand to show a grazed and reddened finger.

'I did that opening it. Tell me, Constable — er . . . '

'Parfrey,' he said.

'Was the front door locked?' she asked.

'Yes. Yes, it was.'

'Oh.'

'I'll be off, then.'

But he hesitated on the threshold.

'This face, was there anything . . . did it look like anyone you know?'

'No. No. Certainly not.'

'I see. Tell me, is Mr. Follett going to be joining you or are you going to be by yourself for the rest of your stay?'

'No. I'll be by myself, I mean. My husband isn't coming,' said Emily, stopping herself from inventing some pointless domestic reason for her husband's absence, and wishing she had introduced herself by her maiden name and status. But it had seemed oddly wrong to misinform the police. And she'd been too shaken for clear thought, anyway.

'Well, good night, then.'

She closed the door and sensed him standing outside till the wards of the lock clicked and the bolts scraped home. She heard his footsteps over the cobbles for a moment, then silence.

One last thing before going to bed. She hunted around through various drawers till she found a couple of drawing pins. Standing on her bed, she pinned the central pages of the *Daily Mail* over the internal window, then squatted with Cal at the foot of the bed to view the effect.

The Chancellor of the Exchequer looked benevolently down at them.

Satisfied, she nodded.

'You I don't mind.'

But she still felt uneasy as she slid back under the single sheet which was all the warm night demanded. Should she have told Parfrey everything about the face? How could she, though? He seemed doubtful enough about its existence, as it was. He probably suspected some kind of hysterical nightmare.

He would hardly have been reassured if she had told him the face was green.

3

When sleep finally came it came solidly, and it was ten o'clock in the morning when she awoke. It would have been later, but Cal, having obviously from the state of the curtain made a vain attempt to leave by the window, applied himself vigorously to washing her face with his tongue.

It was another glorious day, already growing very hot. The Scottish shore of the Solway was perfectly clear. The smoke from Chapel Cross cooling towers was rising perfectly straight into the air. Distance removed any sense of pollution.

A line of small boats was moving slowly against the tide which wasn't much past full. They were shrimpers, she knew. She could see the steam rising from the boilers in which the fresh caught shrimps were boiled on the spot.

She breakfasted rapidly on grapefruit juice and a buttered roll, then went out to join Cal who was already down at the water's edge waiting for the stick which was the incentive he needed to plunge into the cool blue water.

'You don't have to wait, you know,' said Emily, as he barked impatiently at her. 'If you want a bath, just jump in.'

He barked again. She leaned back and flung the stick she had brought with her far into the water. It had once been an Indian club, but Cal's enormous jaws had crushed a great deal of shape out of it.

Emily waited till she saw where he was going to land, then moved quickly away. The first shaking from Cal's coat was like a water-cannon's jet. Boisterously he slithered over the shingle towards her and dropped the stick at her feet. He wasn't one of those stupid dogs who bring back a stick then refuse to give it up to be thrown again. This time drops of water flew off the club as it soared through the air, and they glistened in the sunlight like a trail of slow sparks.

About a hundred yards further along the shore a small group of people was standing. With a slight shock she recognised the uniform and the slim figure of Constable Parfrey. Her first thought was that he must still be investigating the break-in (though what was broken?) in her cottage the night before. And she felt illogically annoyed that her walk might be spoilt by a renewal of questioning. She toyed with the idea of turning away towards the grassy paths of the Grune, but another familiar figure now detached itself from the group and began to move towards her.

It was Burgess.

She expected him to be full of concern for her safety, but nothing of this showed in his greeting.

'Hello there! Taking advantage of the weather? Sleep well?'

'Why yes. Or rather, yes and no.'

But before she could go on to give an account

of her adventure he jerked his head at the group he had left.

'More excitement there, I'm afraid.'

'Oh?' she said coolly, though fully aware of the absurdity of her pique. 'What's the matter? Has someone caught a fish?'

'Nothing like that,' he laughed. 'No. I don't quite know what to make of it. It's our friend Fenimore. He's gone missing again.'

'Oh no!' Now she was really interested.

'Well, according to Amanda, he feels the heat terribly. I can believe her! And last night it was very stuffy. She's been playing hell about lack of air-conditioning in the hotel. She's sure the place is controlled directly from Red China via a front organisation in Carlisle. Anyway, Fenimore got up in the middle of the night announcing he was taking a little walk to cool off and that's the last she saw of him.'

'Didn't he come back?'

'Not that she knows. Amanda went to sleep again, woke alone in the morning and just assumed he'd gone on down to breakfast. When the waiters told her he hadn't, she began to worry and began to re-create the scene you saw last night. The manager finally lost his cool, and the good lady thereupon telephoned the police.'

'Hence Constable Parfrey.'

'That's right.' He looked at her quizzically. 'You know him?'

'A little. Go on.'

'Well, so far, so amusing. Parfrey arrived, and the rest of us all sat back waiting for Fenimore to make another dramatic entrance. But he didn't.

Instead old Chambers, one of the permanent residents, returned from his morning walk carrying a gaily striped T-shirt which Amanda immediately identified as her husband's. He'd come across it on the shore just at the high-water mark.'

He began to move back to the group, but Emily remained where she was.

I don't want to go there, she thought. Not where there's worry, concern, fear. I haven't come here for that. Last night was enough for me.

Burgess stopped and looked back at her enquiringly, then grinned as a sudden squall of rain hit her. It was only Cal, returned once more with his club between his teeth.

But this time he had brought something else. He often did this. He would make straight for the club, but if anything else swam into his ken he would happily grab it in his capacious jaws as a kind of bonus. Usually it was a piece of driftwood or some other common flotsam.

This was different and Emily's stomach turned over as she looked down at it.

This was a shoe.

Burgess saw her face and moved quickly back to her. He bent and picked it up.

Cal barked for attention, but Emily ignored him. Burgess peered into the shoe.

'American make,' he said. 'Come on.'

Now she had no choice but to follow.

For some reason she had assumed Amanda was not in the group who now turned and watched their approach. She would have

41

expected to hear her voice even if she couldn't see her. But now as the men (Parfrey, Roberts, the hotel manager, and two others she vaguely remembered having seen at the bar last night) turned they parted with unconsciously theatrical timing to reveal Amanda seated on the sun- and water-bleached core of a tree trunk left by some old and violent tide.

The only times I've seen her she's been worried about her lost husband, thought Emily with a touch of frivolity which disappeared rapidly as she got a good look at the woman. She looked physically deflated. She was obviously nearer sixty than the fifty Emily had guessed. The gaily coloured floral print dress she was wearing seemed to hang loosely on her, and its brightness acted as a foil to the pale deep lined haggardness of her face. One hand played nervously with a large cameo locket which hung round her neck while the other trailed loosely down to the sand clutching an obviously forgotten cigarette.

She looked up at Emily and made a brief gesture of acknowledgment, then returned to peering out to sea.

'Good morning, Mrs. Follett,' said Parfrey. Emily glanced at Burgess to see how he reacted to this form of address, but his face did not change at all. He was either very resistant to surprise or — and this seemed more likely — he was so concerned with the business in hand, he didn't notice.

'How are you this morning?' Parfrey went on. 'None the worse for your adventure?'

Now Burgess did look surprised.

'I'm fine, thank you, Mr. Parfrey,' said Emily.

'Good.'

'Constable,' began Burgess, holding out the shoe. Emily nudged him sharply and flickered her eyes warningly at the fat American woman. Burgess nodded and, taking Parfrey by the elbow, began to move away with him. But Amanda was not as bemused as she seemed and now looked up.

'What's that?' she said sharply. 'What's that you've got there?'

Burgess hesitated, but Parfrey took the shoe from him and held it out for Amanda to see.

Her examination took only a few seconds. The pause that followed it was longer.

'It's his,' she said. 'It's been in the water.'

There was a flatness about her voice which Emily recognised as the calm at the centre of hysteria.

If she cries, I'll slap her face, she thought. But this. What can I do for this?

No one spoke. It was Parfrey's job to do something, she felt, but Parfrey, she noticed, seemed to be watching the others with calm interest, waiting for them to act.

A diversion came.

'Look,' said the oldest of the men there, Mr. Chambers, she guessed.

He pointed along the beach towards the Point. Cantering along the sand through the shallows came a huge black horse, beating up such a spray with its hooves that at this distance it seemed to belong as much to the water as the land. It was a

43

magnificent sight and Emily felt a surge of envy of the rider, who seemed for a moment to have as little connection with the sorrows and problems of humanity as the great beast he rode with such grace.

Then she remembered the hoofprints which had circled her sleeping body the previous day. And with a surge of anger she knew who it was even before he came within recognition distance.

'It's that fellow Scott,' said Chambers.

'Can he help?' cried Amanda. 'Perhaps he's seen something. He knows these parts well, they reckon.'

Emily wondered who 'they' were and why the Castells had been talking about Scott, anyway.

'Perhaps,' said Chambers, obviously glad of any kind of action.

'Hey, Scott!' he cried, his high-pitched old man's voice being projected with surprising power.

For a moment it looked as if Scott was going to ignore them, then he reined back his horse and came to a standstill about twenty yards away at the edge of the receding tide.

'Yes?' he said.

Something stirred on the saddle in front of him and he put down a soothing hand.

It was the cat which had so savagely offered to do battle with Cal the night before. The big dog, who had settled down patiently on the stones to wait for a resumption of his morning walk and game, now stood up growling deeply in his throat.

'Steady,' said Emily.

Obviously Scott was coming no closer. Parfrey still held his peace and it was Burgess now who, after glancing at Amanda, began to move over the shingle towards the rider.

If his intention was to achieve some privacy from the hearing of the rest, especially Amanda, the stillness of the morning and the clarity of Scott's speech defeated him.

'We're a bit concerned about Mr. Castell, the American at the hotel, you'll remember him. Have you seen anything of him this morning? Earlier?'

'No.'

The answer did not invite further intercourse, but Burgess pressed on, lowering his voice, but still audible.

'We found a piece of clothing of his, you see, back there. Just on the high-tide mark. And a shoe.'

Now his voice dropped below the audibility mark, and Emily could not catch more than the interrogative note on which he ended.

Scott sat quite still for a moment, then turned in his saddle and appeared to examine the sea.

'If the shrimpers don't net him, try Blitterlees or Wolsty Bank at the next tide,' he said.

A pressure of the knees and the trio, cat, man, and horse, all clothed in black, moved off down the shore. He did not look back at them as he went.

Amanda Castell was standing now, her hand at her mouth.

'The bastard, the bastard!' exploded Emily. Cal ran forward a few paces after the horse and barked fiercely. Burgess began to walk back towards them and Parfrey seemed to reawaken to his official role.

'Mrs. Castell,' he said, 'I don't think there's much more we can do here. I suggest we return to the hotel. Mrs. Follett, perhaps you wouldn't mind . . . '

'Of course,' said Emily. 'Come along now.'

She put her arm round the American, who without a word let herself be led back along the beach towards the hotel.

* * *

She stopped in the hotel only the minimum amount of time it took to see Amanda settled.

There had been a look of desperation in her eyes which Emily shuddered to recall as she resumed her interrupted walk. Somehow she did not feel able for the moment to face the sea again, and despite weighty nudgings and plaintive barks from Cal she kept to the path which wound over the stretch of grass and gorse between the foreshore and the farmland.

At first her mind was full of what had just taken place. She felt that somehow she had just attended at the destruction of a human personality, a destruction almost as complete as that of Fenimore Castell. If he were dead, which seemed certain.

But how? Why? she asked herself. Could he have been stupid enough to strip off and go swimming alone in the middle of the night? But why stupid? For all she knew he was an ex-all-American swimming champion or some such thing. He had been huge, but huge, she now recalled, with muscle that was no longer put to use rather than the fat of self-indulgence. How did he drown, then? Now she was being stupid. Heart attack. Remember the pills. Cramp. Even mere over-confidence. All killers in water. She was a strong swimmer herself, but she felt vicariously afraid as she thought of Fenimore Castell's huge body turning helplessly over and over in the Solway's currents. Then the fear was replaced by a more direct, personal explosion of anger at the recollection of Michael Scott's callous answer to Burgess.

'The swine!' she said aloud.

The sound of her voice brought her back to where she was. Cal looked round hopefully, then resumed his scavenging forays through the undergrowth. She had come quite a way, about a quarter of a mile, without noticing an inch of the ground she was walking over. But now, as she consciously shut her mind to the welter of disturbing emotions which had occupied it, she found that her surroundings accelerated the cooling-down process considerably and soon she was enjoying them with almost unadulterated pleasure.

On either side of the path banked low was a confusion of wild roses, pink and white and red; gorse, bramble, and free-growing bracken. Everywhere she looked foxgloves, four, five, even six feet in height, and white or reddy-purple in colour, rose triumphantly above the tangle below and shook their bells down at it. The heat of the day brought out all the smells of July and soon the hotel with its tragedy, not to mention the cottage with its night visitor, seemed more than the half-mile or so they were behind.

One smell sweeter than any of the others drifted towards her, and looking round she spotted the source: a large honeysuckle bush, its branches yellow with a profusion of blossoms. Emily found herself touched by the urge to break off a small branch to put in her bedroom, but approach from this side was practically impossible. The wisp of a dress she was wearing afforded no protection at all.

The only hope of getting at the honeysuckle, she decided, was to work her way round to the back of the undergrowth before her and see if there was a less-dangerous avenue of approach open there. But working her way round to the back was not very easy either, she found. It was another fifty yards before a possible opening appeared to her right.

'Earn your keep,' she said to Cal, pushing him forward. 'Blaze me a trail.'

She had only taken a few steps, and was already crouching low to avoid an arch of bramble, when a sound made her stop short. It was the clink of metal on stone. But it was its closeness that was really surprising.

She listened carefully. Nothing, except the buzz and hum of a variety of insects many of which were now beginning to pay her all kinds of unwelcome attentions.

Then it came again, twice in close succession. The sound of someone digging.

Suddenly she didn't like it all. Didn't like the sound. Or the place. Or her own awkwardly bent position. I can do without honeysuckle, she told herself. It probably wouldn't last anyway.

She began to put herself into reverse, but Cal, sensitive animal though he was, missed the nuances of her thought here, and as soon as she started to move again, albeit backwards, he pressed on ahead as he had been instructed.

'Cal!' she hissed. There was a long silence, broken finally by the clink of metal on stone again, presaged this time by the just audible thud of metal into earth. And followed almost immediately by a loud inquisitive bark.

'And what have we here?' said a man's voice, precise, with a note of academic curiosity. And apparently very close.

Emily shrugged at her own misgivings and set off in pursuit of Cal. Only a few yards round the next bush she found the narrow track she was following opened into a small glade. Along one side of it ran a ridge of newly distributed earth above a recently dug ditch into which Cal was peering with all a dog's interest in excavation. Standing looking at him with a spade in his hand and contriving to look very cool in his tweedy suit was Mr. Inwit or Mr. Plowman. And standing behind him in his boiler-suit with a trenching tool in his hand was Mr. Plowman or Mr. Inwit.

'Hello,' said Emily brightly. 'Is this where it's all happening then?'

'Where what is all happening?'

It was the thin scholarly-looking one in the

boiler-suit who spoke, the same voice she had heard before.

'Where your archaeological research is all happening,' said Emily politely, but could not resist going on: 'and what we have here is a dog. My dog. Here, Cal.'

Obediently the big animal positioned himself behind her and yawned, showing his solid, gleaming white teeth and apparently several yards of moist red throat.

Tweedy-suit put the blade of his spade down carefully and laughed.

'You'll have to stop being so pedantic, Inwit. Else you'll start to fossilise inside.' He laughed again.

So Boiler-suit is Inwit, thought Emily. That makes you Plowman. You look quite jolly, really. Not like your friend. He looks as if you'd just dug him up.

Her eyes strayed to the ditch.

'Well, you know about us then, Miss . . . ?'

'Salter,' interjected Emily, wondering how people would regard her new two-name status now Parfrey was going around referring to her as Mrs. Follett. Not that it mattered. Another few days and she'd be off. One way or another, she'd leave. Where? Somewhere. It was like the emptiness over the edge of a cliff. She shut her mind against it.

'Are you interested in archaeology?' Plowman went on, his bright little eyes twinkling in his rosy-cheeked face.

He looks more like a well-to-do farmer than a ploughman, thought Emily.

'A little,' she said with an answering smile.

'How lucky we've been, eh, Inwit,' he said over his shoulder. 'First that splendid American gent who not only listened, but dug. And now Miss Salter. Not that we'll try to make you dig, my dear. Ha ha ha!'

'Oh dear,' said Emily, reminded of the morning's events, but reluctant to be the bearer of bad news. 'What you said — about Mr. Castell, I mean — it reminded me. Haven't you heard?'

Inwit shook his head jerkily. His expression had not changed, but considerable concern was etched on his companion's ruddy features.

'He's missing again,' said Emily. 'And they found a shirt that was his lying on the beach.'

'You mean he's been drowned?' said Inwit, a flicker of interest on his face now.

'No, no, no, Inwit. You jump too quickly to the worst conclusions. Miss Salter didn't say that at all. We would be wrong to assume that on such slender evidence.'

Emily was quite touched by Plowman's obvious determination to be as hopeful as possible, probably for her own benefit. But she shook her head slowly at him.

'I'm afraid there is other evidence. A shoe, there was a shoe, one of his, floating well out in the water. He might be wandering around without a shirt, but hardly without his shoes.'

'A shoe?' said Inwit, with a slight edge of surprise.

'Yes. Cal here, my dog, he found it.'

'Did he now?' said Inwit. 'That was

51

exceedingly perspicacious of him.'

He moved forward as if to pat Cal, but the dog growled softly and he stepped back again.

'This is most distressing, most distressing,' said Plowman wiping his brow with a large khaki handkerchief. 'How can it have happened? How? That poor man. And his wife. She must be suffering tremendously. I only met her very briefly last night, but it was obvious she adored Mr. Castell.'

He turned with sudden decision to his companion.

'Inwit,' he said, 'I don't feel able to carry on here for the moment. Perhaps you wouldn't mind tidying up while I go back to the hotel to see if I can be of any service. If you're going back that way, Miss Salter, it would be an honour to accompany you. You don't mind, old fellow, do you? I'll see you later. Come along, Miss Salter.'

Emily found herself being propelled back along the track she'd entered by.

'Off you go, Cal,' she said to the dog, which trotted ahead once more.

'Good morning, Mr. Inwit,' she called over her shoulder, but the taciturn half of the partnership was already working at the trench again and did not look up. It was only a brief glimpse she had through a trellis of briar and grasses, but she got a distinct impression that he was filling it in.

Out in the open again she shook back her hair and picked a few bits of vegetation off her dress.

'Just what are you looking for in there, Mr. Plowman?' she asked. 'It's a bit off the beaten track, isn't it?'

'Ah, I see your problem,' laughed Plowman. 'What specifically are we looking for, and is it in the middle of that clump of gorse and briar? Well, the answer is nothing and no. Ha ha ha. Inwit would disapprove if he heard me talking like this. He looks upon archaeology as a science. To me it has more of the qualities of an art.'

Mr. Plowman seemed to have shaken off his initial fit of despondency at the news of Castell's disappearance and was now striding out obviously enjoying the air.

'But what are you looking for?' insisted Emily. To her surprise he began declaiming:

'For wonder of his hwe men hade,
Set in his semblaunt sene;
He ferde as freke were fade,
And oueral enker grene.'

'*Sir Gawain*, isn't it?' said Emily. 'And the Green Knight?'

'Good! Marvellous! Then you know it?'

'I did English at university for a while,' said Emily.

'A pretty girl with a degree! How fortunate a meeting this has been.'

'No,' corrected Emily. 'No degree. I never finished the course. But what's Gawain got to do with Skinburness? I remember Carlisle was once posited as a possible site of Camelot, but I thought Cadbury had everyone's vote now.'

'Perhaps. But it's not that. No, there was also a theory now generally discredited that the Green Chapel in *Sir Gawain* could have been situated here, near Skinburness. The Chapel of the Grune, you see. Or rather you hear, eh? Ha ha ha. No one important thinks there's anything in it now. But me, I like it. It's just the spot. Do you remember how Gawain finds the chapel on New Year's morning? And he stands there, looking around for any sign of life? Then suddenly a sinister sound breaks the silence.

'What! hit wharred and whette, as water at a
  mulne;
What! hit rusched and ronge, rawthe to
  here!

'It's the edge of the Green Knight's axe being sharpened on a grindstone! That's what I'd love to find here. Eh? Imagine turning up a medieval grindstone! I don't dare say such things to Inwit! And even if I did find one he'd offer some perfectly reasonable explanation for its presence. Which would probably be true. But I'd let him feed his learned journals with it. I'm on holiday and it's food for the imagination I want.'

They had reached the track which led up to the hotel and Emily halted there. The look of high-spirited enthusiasm which had been on Plowman's face as he talked now faded. 'Well, I must be off to see that poor woman,' he said. 'It's been a pleasure talking to you, my dear.'

'For me too,' she said. 'The Green Knight. Why was he green?'

'Oh that.' He laughed. 'Green is a fairy colour, isn't it? It's the colour of vegetation and most of our English mythology is vegetative in origin.

Things which are dead come back to life. The Knight loses his head, but picks it up again. Hence most of our fairies, bogies, elves, goblins and what have you, if they're any colour at all, they're green. So don't stop to talk to any green men, my dear, will you? Goodbye for now.'

Chuckling again, he set off towards the hotel. As she watched him go, Emily realised he had still not really told her why he was digging in the middle of a thicket. Now she remembered Fenimore Castell's return to the hotel the previous evening. He too had announced he'd met Inwit and Plowman in the middle of a clump of gorse and fern.

Perhaps they're just a pair of particularly shy archaeologists, she told herself.

Cal snorted, apparently in disdain. But Emily recognised the sound as a demand for his midday snack of about a pound of dog meat.

'All right,' she said. 'I could stand a lettuce leaf myself. But this afternoon, mark you, I'm just going to lie in the sun and not talk to a single soul!'

★　★　★

She kept her promise to herself, though not without difficulty. There were several people on the shore near the spot where Fenimore Castell's shirt had been found. At first she thought they were just staring with ghoulish aimlessness at the sea, but on looking herself she saw a helicopter far out and low over the water. Her heart sank; she knew they could only be looking for a body now, and she felt vaguely guilty as she kept to the inland paths to avoid meeting anybody.

She didn't stop until she reached the Point itself. Here there was no one and as always the place gave her a feeling of great remoteness, though there were plenty of signs of human activity. There was a small pill-box, a remnant of the war years when the whole shore had been controlled by the military. She clambered up on its grass-covered roof and leaned on the rough stone cairn which had been built there.

To her right lay Skinburness Creek where the English fleet had once been anchored. Now there were a couple of sailing dinghies lying askew on the shore and an old rowing boat around which sheep were grazing.

Out over the water to her left she could see the tall masts which rose above the village of Anthorn, distant sisters of the ones at Caerlaverock over the water. There was some kind of naval research station there too, she knew, but was very vague about its purpose.

Something moved suddenly below her, and, startled, she swung round. But it was only a sheep. Cal's ancestral ghosts stirred him to jump down and give the animal a gentle butt with his head which sent it scurrying off.

Emily laughed at the sight, but admitted the fright to herself.

Your nerves are a bit thinly stretched, she told herself. Treatment: Stage one: Sunshine and rest.

She jumped down and picked out a grassy spot overlooking the Firth. Then, after taking off her towelling wrap and anointing every inch of her body except the small area covered by her bikini, she stretched herself out and went to sleep.

When she awoke it was late in the afternoon and Cal had disappeared again.

She spent a fruitless half-hour wandering around, calling for him.

'Damn! Damn! Damn the animal!' she said. 'This is getting to be a habit.'

Putting her wrap on and running a comb through her hair, she set off back towards the village.

I've been too soft with him lately, she thought angrily. Just because I made such a fuss of him yesterday, when he did this, he thinks he'll try it again. We'll see, my lad. We'll see!

Her suspicions were confirmed as she approached the cottage and saw the familiar brown and white bulk lying up against the front door.

'Cal!' she called, with every ounce of sternness she could muster. 'Heel, sir! At once!'

Obediently the dog rose and came towards her. Instantly she knew something was wrong. He was moving at a good rate, but nothing like his usual cavalry charge. And he was obviously hanging his left foreleg.

'Cal!' she said, the tone of her voice changing. 'What's the matter, boy? What is it?'

The matter was plain to see when the two of them met.

His Great Dane leg, unprotected by the shag of hair which covered his torso, had three deep parallel claw marks running from just below the quarters to the joint. And there was a thin stain of blood oozing through the hair above his right eye.

Emily felt sick when she saw this. This was his one good eye. A close examination revealed, however, that there was only the slightest of scratches beneath the hair and this was well up over the eye itself.

She whistled with relief when she saw this, but went hot with anger as she looked once more at the gashes on his leg.

'That bloody cat!' she said. 'You big soft dope. You wouldn't hurt a fly and that vicious creature tears you to pieces. I hope you bit its head off!'

Awareness of the contradictions in her speech did not appease her anger. Gently she led Cal into the dark cottage and bathed his wounds. Then 'Scott,' she said, and seized the telephone directory. She was already dialling the first 'Scott' in the book when she remembered what little she knew about the man.

'The college!' she said out loud. 'He's something to do with the college.'

Swiftly she turned to the 'C's'. No college was listed. Similarly under 'S' for Silloth and 'S' for Skinburness there was no college. She thought for a while and then turned to 'Cumberland' and ran her finger down the list of council and other offices. Still no college. 'E' for education was no help either. Finally in frustration she flung the book across the room and dialled the operator.

A young girl answered. Briefly Emily explained her difficulty. There was a long pause. A few seconds later a new voice came over, older, more assured.

'Can I help you, madam?'

'You can start by telling me who you are.'

'I am the supervisor here.'

'Good,' said Emily. 'All I want is a telephone number. I've given your girl the details.'

'Yes. I see. I'm afraid that the number is ex-directory, madam.'

'Look,' said Emily, her original anger against Scott now overflowing into new channels, 'if you're so powerless you can't *give* me the number, perhaps you could dial it for me. Make it a personal call. Say I want to speak to Mr. Scott. That way I'll get my call and you'll keep your precious secret.'

There was another long pause. Emily began to feel she had been unnecessarily rude. But the voice spoke again.

'I'll see what I can do, madam.'

Everything went dead and remained so for so long that Emily became convinced she'd been cut off. She began to joggle the rest.

'Hello,' said a man's voice.

'Hello,' she said. 'Mr. Scott?'

The man ignored her. 'Who is that speaking?' he asked in peremptory fashion.

'Listen,' said Emily, 'is that the college?'

'Who is speaking?' repeated the voice.

'My name is Emily Salter,' she said, deciding that this might be the quickest way to achieve results. 'I would like to speak to one of your staff, a Mr. Scott.'

'What is your business with him?'

Emily snorted with indignation. 'That I think is very much my business.'

'It is a personal matter?'

'Yes. It damn well is.'

'Wait.'

The wait lasted seconds only.

'Mr. Scott is not available. I will ask him to contact you.'

Again the line went dead.

'Why, you ill-mannered bastard!' cried Emily, and began beating a violent tattoo on the rest with her forefinger.

Suddenly another voice spoke clearly in her ear.

' . . . and your brief is to watch. Merely that . . . '

Then the line went dead again.

Emily sat looking at the phone in utter stillness for a while.

'Your call is over now,' said the supervisor's voice. 'Please replace your receiver.'

Without a word, Emily obeyed. Cal came to her and thrust his great head on to her lap.

'Well, Cal,' she said shakily, 'this place is really getting on my nerves. I could have sworn that voice . . . it sounded just like Sterne.'

The dog growled softly at the name and Emily tousled his head. When she felt him wince slightly as she touched the cut over his eye, her quiet mood fell from her.

'Not available, isn't he!' she said with all her former anger. 'Then I'll just make him available!'

Quickly she changed from her bikini into a dress.

'Stay,' she ordered Cal, but he looked at her so reproachfully that she relented.

'All right. It'll stop your leg from stiffening up too much, anyway. But stay close to me!'

Her first thought was to make for the college itself, but as she closed her door behind her, a new idea came into her mind. It was now six o'clock, after opening time. It was not impossible that Scott might already be in the back room at the hotel. In any case, she felt the need for a drink and there was nothing in the cottage.

Outside the smoke-room door she tapped Cal on the head, and obediently he sat down. There was no notice here forbidding entry to dogs, but harsh experience had taught her the dangers of pushing open a bar door and sending Cal in first. Most other dogs kept away from the moving mountain he represented to them, but some seemed to regard his size as a direct challenge.

Tonight it was all right. It was early and there was only one man in the room, but she didn't let Cal follow her, all the same.

The man was Michael Scott.

He looked up as she closed the door behind her. Her intention was to preserve a dignified coolness, but again as on the previous night she felt as though his glance had flicked her aside dismissively, and she found herself trembling with rage.

'Mr. Scott,' she said.

'Yes?' he said, faintly surprised and looking up again from the book he was reading.

'I would like to speak to you.'

'Speak away,' he said coolly. 'Is it a

standing-up speech or a sitting-down speech?'

She ignored this.

'Mr. Scott, that cat of yours has attacked my dog again.'

That sounds ridiculous, she thought, and Scott obviously considered it as such. He laughed shortly, showing even white teeth, very sharp-looking.

'You mean that pit-pony? Yes?'

'It's no joke!' she cried, feeling herself slipping further away from the cool dignity she desired. 'I don't suppose it's any use hoping that a man as insensitive as yourself can understand other people's feelings, but I'd like to try and make mine quite clear. I consider what you said today on the beach about poor Mr. Castell utterly deplorable. And your peeping-tom act and the vicious pleasure you must get out of animals' pain all add up to a pretty unpleasant character to me.'

She really was trembling now, she thought ruefully. She hadn't meant it to come out like that, all mixed up. Especially as it didn't seem to be having the slightest effect on Scott except to cause him slight amusement. It wouldn't take much to bring tears to her eyes, she knew, and rather than risk that she put as much contempt as she could manage into her face and turned to the door.

'Wait,' he said easily. 'How's the monster's leg?'

Triumphantly she swung round.

'You admit it, then! You know he's hurt his leg, so you admit your cat did it!'

'Why, of course she did,' he said equably. 'I didn't realise that was in dispute. Is that him outside? Hey, boy.'

The door whose handle she had turned preparatory to her dignified exit was being pushed against her restraining hand with a series of muffled bumps. Now at Scott's voice there was a thump larger than those previous and Cal's hairy head appeared.

'The thick end of the wedge,' observed Scott. 'Come here, horse.'

To Emily's surprise and dismay, Cal forced the rest of his body through the door and trotted quite happily over to Scott. Worse, he then proceeded to offer his injured leg for inspection.

'That'll do very nicely,' said the dark-haired man, 'though I'd have left the bandage on till tomorrow at least. Stops him being bothered by flies.'

'Bandage?' said Emily.

'Yes,' he said, looking at her. Then he grinned and ruffled the dog's neck. 'Oh, I see. You took it off yourself, did you? I might have known you'd be a lousy patient. Still, a couple of days and you'll be back on the farm as good as new.'

'Let's get this straight,' said Emily. 'You dressed his wound?'

'Of course.'

'Then it was your cat?'

Scott shrugged. 'I suppose there's little chance of convincing you I'd have dressed it no matter what had caused it. But yes, Miranda did it.'

'Well then!' said Emily, sounding triumphant,

but a bit uncertain inside exactly what she was triumphing over.

'Well then what?' he said. 'Listen, Miss whatever your name is.'

'Salter,' she said. 'Emily Salter.'

'There was extreme provocation.'

'What do you mean?'

'Miranda was sleeping and your dog trod on her. That's right. Trod on her. Fair's fair, though, she was buried deep in the grass and he was making a rather cautious investigatory approach to my horse which must be one of the few animals larger than himself he's ever encountered. Anyway, Miranda's like me; if she's awoken suddenly by something twenty times her weight landing on her belly, she lashes out. He should look where he's going. Though he's blind, isn't he?'

He moved a finger delicately in front of Cal's left eye.

'Yes. He is.'

'He's had a nasty knock there, I should say. How did it happen?'

Emily didn't reply. He looked at her stubbornly unresponsive face and shrugged and glanced down at his book once more.

'I'm sorry,' said Emily. 'I didn't mean to be rude. But I'd rather not talk about it. And I'm sorry about what I said about your . . . Miranda.'

He shrugged inconsequently and she felt the prick of her old anger.

'But the rest of what I said still stands.'

Curiously, the return to attack seemed to please him more than the apology, for he now

64

stood up and smiled.

It was the kind of smile 1920 cinema villains used to have, thought Emily. Too cruel to be true. On the screen, anyway.

'I'm going to have another drink,' he said, moving over to the hatch. 'What about you? Or are you joining the nobs next door again?'

You did register me, then, thought Emily.

He tapped a coin on the counter and the barman appeared.

'Well?' said Scott. 'We'll go dutch if you insist.'

'I don't see why, Mr. Scott,' said Emily, making up her mind. 'If I force you to act like a gentleman, some of it may stick. I'll have a gin and tonic.'

That's good Noel Coward stuff, she laughed to herself. I'm glad there's no one else here to hear me.

'What do you do?' she asked on impulse.

'Me?' said Scott. 'Oh I go around savaging animals, insulting women and spying on young girls. Then I come in here at night to count my blessings and play dominoes.'

'I rang the college,' said Emily. 'You make yourselves very unapproachable up there.'

'You got through, did you?' he murmured with slight surprise. 'My, how insistent a young gal you must be.'

But, despite his lightness, some more serious thought had evidently risen in his mind. The barman put the drinks down behind him and coughed lightly, but Scott ignored him. Emily moved forward firmly to pick up her gin.

'Ah, Mrs. Follett,' said a familiar voice.

Standing against the cocktail bar in the next room was Parfrey, and, by his side, Burgess.

'Good evening, Mr. Parfrey,' she said, and gave Burgess a smile. He looked at her with a curious mixture of pleasure and diffidence on his face.

'How is Mrs. Castell?' she asked.

'Resting. Resting. There have been no further developments.'

'Then there can't be much hope?'

'No,' said Parfrey. 'No, I'm afraid not. Well, I must be off. Good night, Mrs. Follett. Lock your doors now.'

'I will,' she said with a faint grin. 'Good night.'

She turned from the counter and was surprised to see that Scott had moved to the door.

He looked at her and shook his head slightly, as though surprised at something in himself.

'Are you going, Mr. Scott?' she asked, glancing at the untouched Guinness on the counter.

'Yes indeed. I must. I must,' he replied, with an edge of irony in his voice she couldn't understand.

'Chalk it up, George,' he called to the barman.

Cal gave a short bark.

'Good night, horse,' he said. 'And a good night to you too, Mrs. Follett.'

Then he was gone.

Am I going silly, thought Emily, as she sat down and sipped her drink. Or was that last farewell full of all kind of ironic stress and innuendo? But why should the revelation that I'm a Mrs. not a Miss send him off into the night like that?

She smiled to herself with little humour. In her small experience the fact of marriage usually seemed more of an attraction to men than otherwise. Experience without the risk of involvement. Almost an invitation, or perhaps a challenge. Unless they knew Sterne, of course.

Unless they knew Sterne.

Three men came in and noisily equipped themselves with beer and dominoes. One of them, a little square man with a brilliant bald head, approached her diffidently.

'I wonder if you'd mind . . . ?' he said.

Emily was puzzled till she realised she was sitting at the dominoes table.

'Of course not.'

She moved to the padded window-seat and felt something beneath her buttocks as she sat down. It was Scott's book. She placed it on the window-sill. The men sat down to their game, leaving a vacant seat.

'He said he'd be in tonight, didn't he, Joe?' said one.

'Aye,' replied the man who'd asked her to vacate the table. 'Ask George if he's seen owt of him, Dan.'

'If you mean Mr. Scott,' Emily found herself saying, 'he had to leave rather suddenly a few minutes ago.'

'Oh,' said the one called Joe. 'You know Michael, do you? Aye, he's got an eye for a pretty girl.'

They all laughed without malice and Emily smiled with them.

Joe gave a glance at the others, then leaned over to her.

'You wouldn't play dominoes yourself, would you, miss?'

'I have played. Yes.'

'Would you care to join us perhaps?'

Emily's first reaction was to say no. But then she shrugged and thought, Why not? She had nothing else to do and it was early yet to be going back to the cottage.

'All right,' she said. 'Just till someone else comes.'

She did just intend to stay a short while. They played a form of four-ended dominoes she was unfamiliar with, paying the winner a penny a spot with a shilling limit. For the first couple of games they broke her in gently, giving a commentary on the play and offering comments on her own dominoes. Then the serious business of the evening began and though there was a continuous exchange of comments and banter, it was a case of no quarter given. Rapidly Emily's losses mounted to fifteen shillings. Then she began to get a grip on things and had reduced the deficit to seven when to her surprise and disappointment 'Time' was called.

'Damn!' she said. It was her 'down' next and she had hoped for another win.

The others laughed.

'You'll come in again, Em?' asked Joe.

'I'd like to, if I may,' she replied.

'May? You must!' said Joe. Then in what might have been meant as an aside to the others or perhaps as a simple compliment, 'You've got to admit it, Michael can pick 'em, eh?'

'Does he pick a great number, then?' asked Emily, straight-faced.

'Ah, that'd be telling!' They all laughed as the group broke up. Scott's book still lay on the window-sill. On an impulse she picked it up and stuffed it into her bag. It would offer an excuse to approach him again, though why she wanted to she couldn't imagine.

Almost unknown to her in her concentration on the game, the bar had become very crowded and there was a great bustle now as people made for the door. There were several faces she recognised. Inwit was there, though he stared right through her with no sign of recognition. Old Chambers too, and one or two other vaguely familiar faces. But not Burgess.

'Come along, Cal!' she said. She had broken her rule tonight and let him stay with her in the bar. He had been very well behaved, though she had had to give him an admonitory jab with her toe when he showed interest in the casual offer of a handful of crisps.

It wasn't till she stepped out into the warm night air and suddenly felt slightly dizzy that she realised all she herself had had to eat since a very light lunch was a couple of crisps. The three or four gins she'd taken would normally have had no effect whatsoever, but now they were jumping around in a very lively fashion in her head. In addition to her surprise she found

69

she felt vaguely amorous. She stretched herself languorously, enjoying the sense of her young and fit body under the flimsy dress, then laughed as a car headlight caught her, and assumed a more decorous pose as she waited for Cal, who was relieving himself against the hotel wall.

I must be a nice object of sexual hypothesis, she thought. Attractive young woman, married, but without her husband, alone in a seaside cottage.

She laughed again. Oddly the thought of being alone in the cottage did not dampen her spirits at all.

Green man, she told herself, if I get my hands on you tonight, I might just eat you alive.

Carefully she ushered Cal along the short stretch of road they had to cover before turning off. Cars from the hotel were roaring away through the night towards Silloth and there was no pavement. But soon they turned into the dark unmetalled lonning which led down to the shore and the sea, and she was able to let go of Cal's hairy mane and send him ahead.

The only light here had drifted millions of miles from the stars. A romantic thought, but not quite true, she told herself. It was just after 10:30, and there was still evidence in the pale blue fringe of the western sky that the sun was not long gone. The moon had still to put in an appearance, but was due pretty soon. From ahead came the constant unhesitating murmur of the sea. A soft breeze was blowing off it, bringing a subtle blend of ozone and the perfumes she had breathed so happily earlier in the day.

'I cannot see what flowers are at my feet,' she murmured, 'nor what soft incense hangs upon the boughs . . . no, that's hardly it. This is much fresher, less confined and stifling!'

She breathed deeply. Ahead she saw Cal's silhouette pause as he reached the bottom of the lane. Left was the cottage, right were the paths along the Grune to the Point.

Again she became very aware of her body beneath her dress. Suddenly the thought of slipping out of her clothes and plunging into the water became very attractive.

You must be mad! she told herself, but at the same moment resolving to turn right and walk along the foreshore far enough to guarantee privacy. Cal would love it, she knew.

The dog seemed to have anticipated her thoughts, for after standing still for a long moment he himself had turned right and moved almost out of sight. She could still see his hind-quarters protruding from the end of the hedge. He seemed to have stopped again.

Then suddenly he was barking furiously and making explosive gasping sounds while he rolled around, thrashing to left and right with all his great strength, on his back.

'Cal!' she called desperately. 'Cal!' And set off running with all the speed she could down the lane.

Her one thought was to get to her dog. Her blonde hair streamed out behind her, one of her sandals flew off, her handbag flew open as it whirled round on her wrist and its contents showered out behind her.

The dog had heeded her cries, for he stood up as she approached, one huge paw brushing desperately at his face. For a second the thought flitted into her mind that perhaps he had stuck his nose into a nest of wasps.

Then as she reached the end of the lane a figure stepped out from behind the line of hedge and with a round arm swing punched her violently in the stomach.

She had often read of attacks on women, assault, rape, and had sometimes marvelled at the ease with which it seemed to have been done. Pridefully she had reckoned that she would give most men a very good fight indeed and on grounds of sheer logic she believed that rape while she remained conscious was impossible.

Now as she collapsed, retching, gasping desperately for breath, her arms and legs utterly unco-ordinated, she knew that she had lost, utterly and finally. Anything could be done to her. There were no powers of resistance left.

But the horrors had only started. A gloved hand was clapped over her eyes and rubbed violently to and fro. She had no breath for screaming, otherwise she would have shrieked so loudly they would have heard her across the Solway. Now she knew what had happened to Cal. Pepper. Rough raw pepper was being rubbed into her eyes.

She felt herself being turned over like a rag doll. Why oh why does anyone want to do this to me? she sobbed inwardly. Her bag was torn from her wrist. There was a second's respite. Then the hands went under her clothes.

Now, she told herself, now it happens. I fancied a man, and now it happens. Blackness began to tide over her mind.

But another part of her thoughts seized upon the physical sensations the greater part of her being was shrinking from. The hands still had gloves on. Rough woolly gloves. Hardly the best dress for sexual assault. And their movements, though they ranged with indiscriminate violence over all parts of her body, were investigatory rather than sensual.

He was looking for something.

It only took him seconds to decide it wasn't on her person.

The hands moved away.

She had almost managed to collect enough breath for a scream. She swung her arm up, feeling delight as she caught his face with her nails, and she opened her mouth to tear the silence apart.

He kicked her lightly in the stomach and the air expelled itself noiselessly from her lungs and her knees came desperately up to her chin again as the struggle to breathe renewed itself.

Her eyes were blinded by tears of pain as well as the pepper, and she could see nothing. But distantly she heard his footsteps moving away, not quickly like those of a man running from a crime, but slowly, deliberately.

Like a man looking for something still.

He's looking for the stuff out of my handbag,

she thought. If he doesn't find what he wants, he'll be back.

A little strength came back to her limbs, not enough to lift her up and carry her away, but enough, had she wished, to turn herself over, to move her wide-gaping mouth away from the clump of grass her face was pressed against. Every time she sucked in air, she sucked in the coarse, rough-edged blades. But she didn't move. Movement might invite another blow in the belly. She had never before realised what a vulnerable part of the body the belly was. So large an area. So soft. So easily yielding. She could not bear another blow in her belly.

The tears streaming freely out of her eyes were carrying some of the pepper with them. Not that she needed pepper to make her cry. She felt as if she might cry forever. But now she could see the grass as well as feel it, taste it.

Still she did not move. She was still in great pain, but it was nothing compared to the initial agony. Now she was aware of other things. The grass first. Then, through it, the sky. Spots of light. Stars. A summer's night. Beautiful. The heavens are full of splendour. Tender is the night. The sound of the sea. A steady subdued noise but full of strength. Like a whispered roar. A late seagull mewed.

Please, please, she prayed, let someone come now. Let someone come down the lane. It's not busy, but a lot of people use it. If I hear someone coming I can scream now. I'll save it till I hear someone coming.

But suppose it's him coming back. How will I

know? How will I know?

With desperate caution she raised her head and tried to focus on the wedge of blackness which was the lane. She saw the lights of a car pass along the main road a quarter of a mile away. They just made her own blackness deeper, physically as well as metaphorically.

But perhaps he had gone. Perhaps she was safe.

Footsteps. Coming down the lane.

Now she was aware she need not have worried about how she would know. She knew all right. With no shadow of a doubt.

It was the attacker coming back.

She was still not ready to run. Not even ready to crawl. But she had to try.

She pushed her body away from the ground with her hands, like an athlete doing a press-up. But her last drop of strength was used in getting herself into a sitting position.

She could see him clearly now, in silhouette at least. He looked huge, outlined black against the star-spotted sky. Anyone would look big from this angle, some small area of stasis in her mind told her. But reason was no defence against the terror his bulk caused in her.

Suddenly another large shape moved forward between herself and the man. Cal, growling deep in his throat, still not recovered, but ready to try again.

Almost contemptuously the man drew a hand from his pocket and shook it over the battering ram of a head which was being thrust massively at him.

Cal's growl turned into an explosive sneeze which in other circumstances she might have found comic. And even in these circumstances she felt a pang of quite unselfish distress as the animal once again began his blind pawing at his face, whimpering in pain and confusion.

Her arms were supporting her strengthless trunk. Her hands pressed hard against the earth, and under the left one she felt the hard smooth surface of a stone. It felt like one of the stones off the beach, all roughness worn away by years of movement backwards and forwards with the tide. Her fingers dug around it, trying to loose it from the earth.

God knows what I'm doing to my fingernails! She found she had time to think.

It was free now. Rather too large for her hand, but it was all she had. Use it as a club! she told herself. As a club!

But her nerve broke again at the sight of the figure now almost straddling her and she flung the stone with all her might.

Left-handed, from a sitting position, it wasn't a bad throw. But not good enough. It struck him on the right shoulder and he clapped his hand to the spot, grunting pain. She couldn't see his face, there was some kind of scarf wrapped round the lower part, but she sensed his features twisted with anger, and drew her knees up to her breast to protect her stomach.

From the gloom which stretched away to the Point another shadow detached itself. The attacker sensed it, paused in mid-blow, and turned, becoming motionless before the figure which moved now out of the edge of darkness.

It stood tall, clad in what looked like a single tight-fitting garment. In its hand was a short ungleaming sword.

Through her still streaming eyes Emily stared fascinated at its face. Whatever colour it was, it wasn't white. If anything it was a dark shade of green.

Far away at the head of the lane she heard someone whistling gently, 'Some Enchanted Evening', and footsteps crunching on the loose pebble surface.

Now she could scream.

Her first high-rising shriek had not yet reached its crescendo when the green man stepped back into the night, her attacker stumbled away awkwardly towards the beach, and the footsteps in the lane broke into a run.

'Emily! Emily!' called a desperately anxious voice.

She did not reply, but let her scream die away to a thin bubbling sob.

'Emily!' he called again, unable to pick her out as she sprawled back in the grass.

'I'm here, Arthur,' she said, almost conversational in her exhaustion.

'Friend, Cal. Friend,' she added to the dog, who though obviously still unable to see was growling once again.

Then, as Burgess knelt beside her and gently raised her from the ground, she found herself weeping, not hysterically, but steadily, copiously, as if it might go on forever.

4

'Your stomach will be a bit bruised and painful for a few days,' said the doctor, 'but there's no permanent damage. Fortunately you're obviously quite fit. Nice strong muscles.'

'They felt like jelly,' said Emily, pulling the sheet up over herself. 'And Cal? What about Cal?'

The doctor laughed.

'He seems to be managing quite well for himself. Mr. Burgess provided him with a bucket of water and he seems happy dipping his head into it, then shaking the surplus off on everything within a radius of twenty feet. But I'll have a look at his eyes and apply a drop of something nice and soothing if he'll let me. Now get some rest. I'll be back to see you in the morning. I'm sorry I took so long getting here, but you came second in a queue behind a motor accident in the town.'

'I'm very grateful to you, Doctor.'

'A pleasure. Good night now.'

He gave a jaunty little wave and left. Emily heard him talking with someone outside, then the door opened again and Cal entered, his good eye rather red and inflamed, but obviously usable. He rested his head on her pillow and she had to roll away from his long red tongue.

Behind him came Burgess.

'Hello,' he said.

'Hello.'

He sat down on the bedside.

'Listen, Emily,' he said. 'I've had a word with Parfrey and, if you don't mind, I'll bed down here for the night, on the sofa next door, I mean. You never know. You might want something.'

'Or somebody might want something from me,' added Emily ironically. 'No, I take your point. I'm very grateful. Please be my guest. Though what Mrs. Herbert upstairs will think I don't know.'

'Good,' he said, standing up.

'Don't go yet,' she said. 'Stay till I go to sleep. I feel safer with you here. It's a long time since I felt safe.'

A wave of self-pity rose in her. It was an emotion she had prided herself on avoiding in the past, but now the circumstances, combined with the lethargy produced by the pills the doctor had made her take, seemed to have broken down all the barriers of pride and self-sufficiency she had been at such pains to erect.

She felt a sudden desire to confide.

Burgess had sat down again. She stretched out a hand to him and he took it and patted it reassuringly.

A bit avuncular, she thought. But that's what I need. A nice, kind, sympathetic uncle-confessor.

She stretched luxuriously and immediately regretted it as her stomach muscles proclaimed their unstretchability

'Are you all right?' he asked, noticing her wince.

'Yes. Fine,' she said. 'Arthur, look, I feel I owe you a bit of an explanation.'

'Don't be silly. You owe me nothing.'

He seemed slightly perturbed.

'All right. Perhaps I don't. But I feel like giving you one. You can forget all about it tomorrow, if you like. I'll probably wish you would. But tonight, well, I feel like giving it.'

She felt his hand go tense on hers and felt that while part of him wanted to sit and listen, other elements in him were urging him to leave.

'You must have thought it a bit odd,' she said. 'You invite a Miss Emily Salter to dinner. The next morning you hear her addressed as Mrs. Follett. Didn't you find it odd?'

'Well, I suppose I did. Yes,' he said hesitantly. 'Though it didn't really bother me.'

'Ah, the attractions of a married woman became evident to you,' she murmured.

'No!' he said in protest, almost in panic. 'Don't misunderstand me, please!'

'Just a joke,' she said, surprised. 'But it's true, Arthur. I am married. Oh yes. Really married. I've been married for nearly ten years. Does that surprise you? Ten years. I was just turned nineteen, in my first year at university, when I met Sterne. That was his first name, Sterne Follett. Don't ask me why. Perhaps his mother had been frightened by an eighteenth-century novel. The name seemed a bit comic first time I heard it. But fascinating too. Intriguing somehow.'

And now the name had long lost its fascination for her. And regained nothing of its

80

comedy in the losing. Nineteen, she heard herself repeat dreamily. I was only nineteen.

The whole story came out like this, as if she too were listening to someone else telling it. And the only piece of concrete reality left to her was Burgess's hand, which she gripped convulsively all the time she talked.

She had met Sterne Follett at a reception after a degree-giving ceremony to which Emily had been taken by a young lecturer. The encounter had seemed accidental, but later, when she knew him better, she had begun to doubt if anything like an accident ever happened to him.

He had received an honorary doctorate that day. He was, she learned (though not from him), a rich man who had been a considerable benefactor of the university since its inception five years earlier. But it was the man himself who at the same time attracted her and made her feel gauche and inadequate. He was in the late forties of his middle age, not tall, but well built and fit looking, his hair still thick and vital, despite the distinguished shadings of grey round the temples. Everything he did was done with a certainty of rightness as unostentatious as it was unquestioning. He even discussed Emily's university work with an expertise which made her feel the woeful inadequacy of her own knowledge.

Finally the Vice-Chancellor had come to bear him away, rescuing him from a boring student, Emily suspected. But to her amazement, before he left, Follett suggested they should continue their conversation the following day over tea in the Marlborough, the town's premier hotel.

Her friends all diagnosed the lowest of motives.

'Not at 4 P.M. in the Marlborough,' she protested.

'Don't be naive,' she was told. 'He'll have them off while you're putting honey on your scone.'

'Next time,' they all said with lugubrious certainty when she reported back that all was still well. 'He's softening you up.'

'Next time' was dinner in the town's best restaurant, famous for its menus, its wines, its expense.

It was perfect. Sterne soon dispelled her initial nervousness with the intense interest in her as an equal he seemed to display. The meal was everything reputation had forecast it would be, the wine like nothing she had ever tasted before.

When they came to leave, Emily had firmly made up her mind that anything he cared to ask of her, he could have. He deserved it. More than that, she was looking forward to it. But again nothing happened. He did not even take her back to the hotel for a brandy as had been half suggested earlier. Instead he drove straight to her hall of residence.

Disappointed, she wondered if something had gone wrong. Then he leaned across and kissed her, just once, not violently, but not chastely either, and let her out of the car.

She didn't go to sleep for hours. She woke up, suddenly convinced that this had been the apogee, and spent the rest of the day in such a depression that her friends couldn't make up their minds whether it definitely had or definitely hadn't happened. But she confided in no one. Even to herself it seemed absurd to be madly in love with a man who did not even seem to want to sleep with her. Then she was called to the phone. Sterne had debated and decided. Cold-bloodedly, she was later able to guess. But not then.

A month later she was married to him. It was a quiet wedding. The only guests from her side were her father, her aunt, his sister, who had looked after them since her mother died six years earlier, and Mary who was her bridesmaid. With Sterne were his best man, Charles Dacre, who, she discovered later, was his personal accountant, the Vice-Chancellor and his wife, and a couple of business friends whose names she never recalled.

She did not go back to university, despite the Vice-Chancellor's sincerely expressed hope that she would complete her course.

It seemed the perfect life that they began to lead together. Sterne's business interests took him all over Europe. Emily had never travelled at all. Within two years of her marriage she had visited every European capital and much else besides.

Their social life moved at a level Emily would have considered far beyond her reach a year earlier. Sterne was at home anywhere and in demand everywhere. Soon Emily became conscious of the gently insistent effort Sterne was making to prod her in the right directions, to fit her for her role of hostess in his house and guest at the tables of others. For a long time, a year or more, she was amused by it, even touched. It seemed a signal proof of Sterne's concern for her, his desire that she should not feel out of things in this new life. Gradually, however, it become irksome. She bore with it for long after it had become unbearable. Perhaps this was a mistake. Complaints should be voiced long before they have become angry outbursts.

One evening Sterne handed her a list of guests at a luncheon party they were attending the following day. Casually he began to talk about them, reminding her of those she had already met, telling her things about those who would be new to her.

She listened for a few moments, then rose, sensing her own irritation and sensing the comparative innocuousness of the provocation.

'I'll have the second lesson in the morning, dear,' she said. 'I'm going up to bed now.'

He put the list down and rose courteously to his feet to open the door for her.

'Good night, my dear,' he said.

It was the courtesy which idiotically triggered off the final outburst.

It all came pouring out, first the anger, then the half-apology, then the appeal. He didn't say a word but held the door open. She thought she saw a look of contempt flit over his face.

'Good night, my dear,' he said again.

She went to bed. It had been their first quarrel, she thought absurdly, and was still young enough, or old enough, to be able to laugh at the title.

They had been married nearly three years. It wasn't bad going.

It took another two years for her to admit that her husband was a stranger to her. It was small comfort to look back and think that perhaps he always had been. The discovery that he was also sleeping with a variety of other women hardly came as a shock to her any more than reading the news about a stranger in a divorce-court case. It mattered as little to her as she knew it mattered to him. It could hardly be called 'having an affair' with even the shallow putting-down of roots that that phrase implied.

'You do it to be polite,' she told him, with hardly a jeer in her voice. She had felt constrained by convention to confront him with her knowledge. He didn't deny it any more than he had attempted to conceal it.

'No,' he replied after consideration. 'I do it out of necessity.'

Which either meant he was a sexual maniac or something quite enigmatic.

'So I decided to leave the bastard,' said Emily, suddenly quite loudly.

Burgess, who had been listening to her voice die down and had begun to hope she was sleeping, started in his chair.

'Hush,' he said. 'Don't try to talk any more.'

'What's the matter? You embarrassed, Arthur? A man of the world like you?'

'Go to sleep now,' he said.

'Do you know how long it took me to leave

him? Once I'd made up my mind finally and definitely, I mean? You'll laugh when I tell you. Three years and a bit. Are you laughing? How's that for decisiveness?' she asked drowsily.

'Don't talk,' he repeated.

'You're trying hard to shut me up, Arthur. I thought you had a sympathetic ear. But you needn't listen. I'll just go on talking anyway. I don't know what happened. I was just perfect for the part, I suppose. All that training. When I shouted at him about it, it was too late. I was already word perfect. I could get by without an effort. The hostess with the mostest. When you're gliding along like I was, three years is nothing. Zip! There she goes. And where does she go, anyway? Daddy was dead by then, two years after we got married. I'd lost sight of all my old friends, and the new lot, well, they didn't know what was going on behind my charming smile, so why should I know about them?'

She almost nodded off this time. Burgess rose quietly to his feet. Her voice suddenly grew strong again.

'But I've made it now. Made it. Almost. Just one more . . . and I've made . . . '

Her breathing became slow and even. Gently he switched off the light and gently went out of the room. The old door wouldn't shut without a protesting squeak.

Emily turned slightly in her bed, just below the surface of consciousness again for a moment. She thought she heard a distant ping, like a telephone being lifted off the stand, and a voice speaking low. But if there was anything there at all it was too weak, too distant, to hinder her long, steep slide down into darkness.

She slept.

* * *

Next morning Emily felt far worse than she had done the night before. In fact when she awoke she had felt a peculiar sense of well-being, but as she stretched herself, preparatory to getting up, this feeling disappeared beneath a deluge of aches and cramps which left her weak and miserable.

Carefully she pulled the sheet down and looked in dismay at the large area of bruising round her navel. A tap on the door made her end her survey.

'Come in,' she said.

Suppose a big green man walked in with his head underneath his arm?

The thought was ludicrous enough to make her smile. None the less it was a comfort to see Cal raise himself lazily from the mat at the foot of the bed and amble shaggily doorwards to greet the newcomer.

It was Burgess carrying a tray replete with coffee-pot, cup, grapefruit, and toast.

' 'Morning,' he said cheerily. 'I've trespassed on your larder.'

'Your trespass is forgiven,' she said. 'What time is it?'

'Just after eight. I heard the bed creak, so I thought I'd give you a try before pushing off. I'm going to pop up to the hotel now for a shave and a bath.'

'Oh, you might take Cal with you and send him for a gallop along the shore. He's a creature of regular habits.'

'Right.'

Burgess went to the door, but hesitated there as if there was something else he wanted to say. Finally it came out, a little over-casual.

'That chap you were with in the back bar last night. He was the one with the cat, wasn't he?'

'Yes. Mr. Scott.'

'I didn't realise you knew him. I mean, you didn't seem very friendly towards each other on the other occasions he's appeared.'

'No. I don't suppose we did.'

She stopped herself from adding anything in the way of explanation, feeling a little put out at Burgess's probing and feeling at the same time a little guilty at her resentment. He had been very kind.

'Right, then,' he said finally. 'I'll be on my way.'

'Right,' she said, adding as a kind of atonement: 'And, Arthur, thanks a lot. I seem to recollect beating your ear with all my troubles last night. I'm sorry. Do me a favour. Forget them, will you?'

He nodded, and left.

She surprised herself by eating her breakfast with a good appetite and then settled back with a cigarette to take a long view of the previous night's events.

First, she told herself, it wasn't me he was

after, which may not be flattering, but it is something of a relief. No, it was something he thought I had. What might he think I had? The only thing that comes to mind is Michael Scott's little book. Which is absurd. Who'd want to go pretty near to murder to get hold of something its owner valued so little as to leave lying around a hotel bar without making the slightest effort to retrieve it? And if it was the book, it means that Gentleman Jim who beat me in the gut last night knew I had it. Therefore Gentleman Jim was in the hotel bar last night.

Which brings us to item two. Who is Gentleman Jim? Obviously he's someone who can appear in the hotel bar without causing comment, but at the same time he's some kind of professional thug.

She thought this one over for a while, a trifle surprised at her own conclusion then nodded in agreement with herself.

No one could dispose of me and my dog with such economy of effort who wasn't well practised. Am I being vain? No, she decided, I'm not. Most people would have shied right away from the thought of tackling Cal and would have made a messier job of dealing with me. Perhaps I should be thankful he wasn't just an enthusiastic amateur. Anyway. So what's pro thug doing in a quiet place like this?

And item three. Who is this green man who keeps on popping up out of the ground? Was he for me or against me last night? He didn't really have time to make his intentions clear.

She shuddered. If she had to put Gentleman

Jim and the Green Man in order of preference she would find it very difficult. At least the latter hadn't physically harmed her. Yet.

Plowman's talk of the Green Knight and fairies and vegetation myths came back into her mind. Even now with daylight outside her window she could feel the truth of what he said. Myth, legend, fear and fantasy would find a ready breeding ground here where sea and land met in such an uneasy marriage.

She picked up her history from the bedside table and flicked through the index pages. There was nothing under 'Gawain' or 'Green', but under the heading 'Superstition' she found a host of references. Idly she turned to the major one.

'Stories of villages lost beneath sand and sea abound and the elements of truth in these stories are discussed elsewhere in this book. But the common progeny of such natural disasters, whether real or legendary, appear here too. Bells that toll under water; great gnarled trees brought ashore from submarine forests on the neap tides; houses visible fathoms-deep on a clear day and the usual revenants, the bodies of the drowned, often scaly, green, decaying, bringing with them odour of fish and weed.'

Nice, thought Emily. I'm glad I found that in the morning.

She flicked over a few more pages, pausing when the name Wolsty caught her eye. It meant little to her. She had seen it on a signpost on the road between Silloth and Beckfoot. But more recently . . . now she remembered. That man,

90

Scott, from his god-like elevation on that great black horse, saying coldly, impersonally, 'Try Blitterlees or Wolsty Bank at the next tide.'

Her old anger flared briefly. To quell it, she read on.

'And considering the ignorant and superstitious nature of the people of this area, whose lack of religion caused the authorities much concern, it is not surprising that so many fables and legends should abound, and mustard seeds of truth be swollen into huge shady trees of superstition.'

Nicely put, thought Emily approvingly. They don't write like that any more:

'For instance Wolsty Castle, built as a defence centre for the Abbey of Holm Cultram, served forces other than those of official religion; for in it, according to tradition, were preserved the magic books of the famous Border scholar and, by implication and reputation, wizard . . . '

She turned over the page.

' . . . Michael Scot.'

'Well now,' said Emily aloud. 'That *is* interesting!'

There was a knock at the door.

'Come in,' she called, expecting to see Burgess enter. Instead Cal pushed his way in, very damp, having obviously found someone to throw his stick or having perhaps acted independently in his mistress's absence. And behind him came the man whose name she had just read.

Absurdly, she clutched the sheet up to her throat. He stood at the door looking, for him,

91

remarkably ill-at-ease. Cal had no such inhibitions and placed his forepaws on the bed, which creaked ominously. Forgetting her sheet, Emily pushed him off with mock annoyance.

'Cal, a dog of your size should behave with more dignity. And you're soaking wet!'

'That's my fault,' said Scott. 'I met him on the shore and he practically terrorised me into throwing a stick into the sea for him.'

'You really should be careful who you terrorise, Cal,' she said reprovingly to the dog.

'May I come in?' asked Scott.

'As you seem to have penetrated the outer defences, I don't see why an unlocked bedroom door should deter you, Mr. Scott. Please step inside.'

He did not close the door behind him but came almost up to the bedside and stood there, still a little awkward.

'Mrs. Herbert, your neighbour, let me in. She knows me. And in any case it was the only way to stop Cal beating the door down with his head.'

It was the first time she had heard him call Cal by his name. The dog gave a distant nod of acknowledgment.

'I was sorry to hear what happened to you last night,' he went on. 'Very sorry.'

Emily looked at him curiously. This seemed out of character. And, oddly, what he was saying sounded more like an apology than an expression of sympathy.

'Thank you,' she said. 'It's kind of you to come to tell me this.'

'How badly were you hurt?' he asked.

'Not bad. I was punched pretty hard in the stomach. It's still rather stiff.'

For a second she felt an impulse to shock him by pulling back the sheet and displaying the bruise. But the conviction of his basic unshockability as much as anything stopped her.

'What did he want?' he asked.

'Gentleman Jim?'

'Who?'

'My attacker. You mean him, what did he want?'

'Yes.'

'I've no idea. Not the obvious thing. My maidenly virtue, I mean.'

'That must have been a blow for you,' he said, more like his old self.

'The only blow to me was a left-arm hook to the solar plexus,' she said. 'That hurt.'

'A left-arm blow,' he repeated.

'Yes. Why? Oh, I see. Left-handed. I never thought of that. Not that it signifies anything, really. He gave the impression of being able to use any limb very efficiently as an offensive weapon.'

'Did he steal anything from you? Anything at all?'

Ah, now we're coming to it, Emily thought with satisfaction. The real reason for your visit. You want to know about your little book. And even you didn't like to appear callous enough to ask outright.

'Not that I know of. I mean I don't know,' she corrected herself. 'I haven't been able to check.'

He looked surprised.

'Why? Was there so much to check then?'

'No, Mr. Scott,' she replied with heavy sarcasm. 'But what little there was was strewn all over the lane, and I didn't feel able to pick it all up last night. I daresay it has been picked up since, by Constable Parfrey I shouldn't wonder. But as it's still a little early for most gentlemen callers, even the police, I haven't been able to discuss it with him.'

'Well, now is your chance, Mrs. Follett,' said a cheerful voice from the doorway. Parfrey stood there, helmet under his arm in the regulation fashion. How long he had been there it was impossible to tell.

In his other hand he carried a small shopping bag. Carefully he placed his helmet on a chair and came over to the bedside.

'Good morning, Mr. Scott,' he said. 'I'm sorry to interrupt.'

'That's all right,' said Emily. 'Mr. Scott just called in to pay his devoirs.'

''Morning, Parfrey,' said Scott, showing no sign of being about to leave.

Parfrey looked at him steadily for a moment, then returned his attention to Emily.

'Now, Mrs. Follett,' he said. 'How are we this morning? Feel up to a bit of talk, do you?'

Emily looked at him in surprise. This was vintage Dixon of Dock Green stuff, quite out of character, she would have said.

All the leopards are changing their spots this morning, she thought.

'Yes. I'm quite well, thank you,' she lied politely. She felt a bit better since her breakfast, but still a long way from fit.

'Good,' said Parfrey. 'Now the first thing is to check if anything was actually stolen from you last night. Mr. Burgess and I did a thorough search of the area last night, particularly the bottom of the lane where your bag burst open. And I've had another look this morning. Here's what I found.'

He dipped his hand into the shopping bag like a music-hall conjuror, looking faintly surprised at the objects he produced.

'Leather purse,' he said. 'Containing four fivers, two pound notes, assorted loose change. Right?'

'I think so,' said Emily.

'A lipstick. A steel comb. A compact, rather bent. It must have hit a stone. A bunch of keys, seven in all. A ball-point pen. Driving licence and insurance certificate in a leather case. And that's the lot. Anything missing, Mrs. Follett?'

Emily thought hard, very conscious of Scott who had been watching Parfrey's performance with a saturnine disinterest.

'I think so,' she said. 'No. Wait. There should have been a small leather-backed notebook with a brass clasp. Belonging to Mr. Scott here.'

'Oh?'

'You left it in the bar,' she said to Scott. 'I picked it up. I was going to give it back to you next time we met.'

She found herself flushing before his quizzical gaze.

'There was no sign of a book, sir,' said Parfrey, looking steadily at Scott.

'It was of no importance,' said Scott. 'Not worth stealing. Certainly not worth this kind of assault. It'll probably turn up in a ditch. The main thing is that Mrs. Follett's all right.'

'Yes, that's the main thing,' agreed Parfrey. 'Perhaps I can have a word with you later.'

'Certainly. You can usually get me in the hotel bar, during hours, of course.'

'Or at the college.'

'Certainly. Yes, of course. At the college.'

Scott again seemed faintly amused.

'Well, good day to you, Mrs. Follett, Constable.'

He left with the easy swiftness of movement Emily had noticed before. Parfrey followed him to the door and held it ajar till the outside door slammed. He stood, as if uncertain whether to go himself, and it was Emily who broke the silence.

'Tell me, Mr. Parfrey. I don't mean this to sound impertinent, and I am in no way dissatisfied, but isn't it usual for a case like this to be handled by a plain-clothes man, someone from C.I.D.?'

He nodded slowly.

'Why yes, it is. Of course it is. And some of our detectives will be wanting to question you. We've just got a very small establishment down here, you see, and H.Q. relies on people like myself to do a great deal of the ground work. But don't worry, Mrs. Follett, in a serious matter like this the full machinery of the law is at your disposal.'

He said it so solemnly that Emily smiled,

96

thinking of the rather olde-worlde style of her Solway history. Idly she picked the book up from the counterpane where it had been lying during the interview. Parfrey took this as a gesture of dismissal and, standing up, went to retrieve his helmet.

Disliking her accidental rudeness, Emily fumbled for something to say.

'Tell me, Constable,' she said finally, holding the book up so he could see what it was. 'Do you know anything about Wolsty Castle?'

'A little,' he said. 'I'm a member of a local archaeological group. When I have the time, that is. There's nothing to see at the site now, except the outline of the foundations and the moat. It was finally knocked down in the seventeenth century. If you like, I could probably put you in touch with someone who knows a great deal more about it than I do.'

'Oh no. No,' she disclaimed. 'No, I just thought that if you were looking for Michael Scott's book that might be a good place to start.'

He looked at her in puzzlement, finally coming across to take the proffered book from her hand.

'Oh,' he said, reading. 'That Michael Scot.'

'Do you know anything about him?' asked Emily.

'A little more than I know about our Mr. Scott,' said Parfrey, then seeming to decide he had gone a little beyond his constabulary brief, he coughed apologetically, as though to obscure the remark.

'I'll be off now, Mrs. Follett. But don't worry.

The matter is being thoroughly investigated. Goodbye.'

'Goodbye,' said Emily.

My, she thought. An archaeological police-man. Everyone seemed to be connected with and searching for the past round here. Except herself. She was seeking to bury it, not dig it up.

But, coming back to Parfrey, she almost felt she could have risked telling him about the green man. He had seemed rather uninterested in the appearance of the second mystery man, even when she hinted there had been some resemblance to the intruder in the cottage.

'Your eyes were full of pepper, Mrs. Follett,' he had said reasonably.

So greenness had not seemed a good topic for discussion.

Strange, Sterne had once said to her, the more sensible a woman is, the greater is her fear of being dismissed as an hysterical woman. Therefore the less sensibly she acts.

How nice, she had replied. How nice to understand everything and yet never feel obliged to act with understanding.

And her reply had seemed as cheap as all her outbursts did in the face of his dignified, detached composure.

Fiercely she turned to her book again. There was little more about Michael Scot except for the suggestion that he was buried in the abbey of Holm Cultram.

So we have his body and his books both, she reflected lightly. But the section on myths and superstitions ended with a glance at place names in the district which, in the suggestive mood in which she found herself, dampened her levity.

'Wolsty' probably derived originally from words meaning the 'wolf's path,' or 'wolf's haunt,' and Skinburness she read with a fascination deeper than the bare, scholarly outline of the etymology involved, when broken down into its three Old English component parts, meant simply 'the headland of the castle of the demon.' She had known this before, but forgotten. She remembered now who had told her. It was Sterne.

5

The rest of the morning went past slowly. The doctor called, prodded her professionally, gave her some pills to take at frequent intervals, and pronounced himself well satisfied.

Mrs. Herbert descended from above with coffee and comfort for a short time, and Emily found herself wishing the old woman had been able to stay longer. Cal was little use as company. He plainly felt they should be out and about and made his feelings clear by letting out occasional reproachful barks and attempting to drag the bedclothes on to the floor.

After one particularly loud bark, she got up, wrapped her robe around her and escorted Cal to the front door.

'Go and find a playmate!' she commanded. 'And for Godsake pick on someone your own size if you're feeling amorous.'

It was nice to be out of bed, but her legs felt surprisingly weak, as if she had been bedridden for weeks instead of a couple of hours. And she found it difficult to walk upright, but inclined forward slightly to ease the ache in her stomach muscles.

She found herself wondering what had happened to Burgess. He had said he would be away for only a very short time. But that was three hours ago and both Parfrey and the doctor had been and gone long since.

Illogically she found herself resenting his absence, as though she had some real call upon his person. Even as she laughed at her own illogicality, she found herself thinking, But he *did* say he would be back quickly. I didn't ask him to. He said it of his own accord.

Finally this childish possessiveness made her try to take a clearer look at her relationship with Burgess. The shadow of Sterne was still too dark over her for her to be able to contemplate entering into any real intimacy with another man. And the hard fact of her marriage, with all the problems of divorce still to face, made this even more undesirable. Sterne believed in bargains. If he did not feel she had kept to hers he would not make things easy for her. That was all she could be certain of. Not that she cared all that much now somehow.

But Burgess now. She liked what she knew of him, though she was sure she did not yet know all of him by any means. She had a distinct impression of him as a man who would have to struggle for any independence he wished to achieve, while the Scotts of this world moved surefootedly on, confident in their own powers and purposes.

The vehemence of her attitude to Scott surprised her once again.

In any case, she thought, decisively, I've had this place. One more night to let the tummy get back into shape, then I'm off, no matter what.

Where to? she asked herself.

Anywhere. Who cares? Somewhere where there aren't any green men spying on me. Or thugs beating me up. So it'll be goodbye, Burgess, and Scott, and Parfrey, and Uncle Tom Cobley and all.

Her thoughts had come full circle and she was about to return to bed and try one of the doctor's little pills when the phone rang.

The sound jarred on her nerves and she snatched the receiver up with unnecessary violence before it could ring again.

'Yes?'

'Mrs. Follett?'

The voice was distant, not so much in physical terms, though it seemed that too; but the speaker sounded detached, far away. As if pitched past some pitch of despair Emily could only imagine.

It was a woman's voice. And familiar for all its strangeness.

'This is Mrs. Follett speaking.'

'Listen, hon, this is Mandy Castell here. I'd like to speak with you if I may, Mrs. Follett.'

'Why certainly, Mrs. Castell,' replied Emily in some surprise. 'What is it you want to talk about?'

The woman at the other end laughed, shortly, without humour.

'No. I mean I'd like to speak with you personally, hon. Could you come up to see me at the hotel?'

'Well, to tell you the truth, Mrs. Castell, I'm a little indisposed at the moment.'

'Yeah. I heard.'

For a moment Emily felt hotly indignant at the woman's demands, knowing as she seemed to what had happened the previous night. Then memory of what had happened to Amanda Castell herself the previous day flowed back into her mind, and indignation vanished.

'It's important, hon. It is to me, at least. And it'd be better if you could come here.'

Emily made up her mind.

'All right, Mrs. Castell. When?'

'Soon as you can, hon. And don't make a noise about it, huh? I mean, you needn't wear a mask, but don't get the manager to page me or anything like that. I'm room 22. First floor.'

'I'll come as soon as I can.'

'See you.'

The phone went dead.

Now what on earth, Emily asked herself as she replaced the receiver, was all that about?

Suddenly she was very intrigued and bustled back into the bedroom to get dressed. She rubbed some of the doctor's balm gently onto her stomach before putting her pants on, but even the pressure of her own fingertips made her wince. Strangely, she felt extremely guilty, as she had done as a child when, confined to her room either to do homework, or as a punishment, she had sneaked out without permission.

And the shock she had always felt when caught in the act by her father or mother was also re-experienced when she quietly opened the front door and almost bumped into Arthur Burgess.

'Well hello!' he said with exaggerated surprise. 'You're up.'

'It's not exactly a case of Lazarus rising,' replied Emily tartly, annoyed at her own fright.

103

'Where have you been?'

She immediately regretted the question. It implied that she had some call upon his time, and special relationships she knew always run two ways.

His reply reassured her to some extent.

'Something came up at the hotel. A personal matter. I had to make some phone calls. Otherwise I'd have been back sooner. But the doctor's been, hasn't he?'

His tone was casual, almost offhand. The warmth of his concern for her the previous night was very well concealed. She was reminded of the way he had seemed to cool off after their dinner at the hotel.

Blow hot, blow cold, I don't care, she told herself. And was amused once more at her own inconsistency.

I want it all ways, she thought. To be adored without being bothered!

'The doctor has been?' Burgess repeated.

'Oh sorry,' she said. 'Yes. Clean bill of health except for a bit of bellyache.'

'Good-oh. If you're going for a walk, I'll join you if I may. I'm still a bit stiff myself from that couch last night!'

'No. I'm going up to the hotel.'

'Oh. The hotel.'

Oh dear, thought Emily. That does sound like another snub. He has been good and does deserve rather better treatment.

'I'm going to pop up and see Mrs. Castell,' she said. 'Perhaps we can have a drink afterwards? My round.'

'Mrs. Castell?' he said.

Emily felt her initial annoyance at his echoing tactics returning.

'I shouldn't bother,' he went on. 'I gather she is resting under pretty strong sedation. There's still no sign of her husband's body. But I'll gladly accept your drink.'

Sedation. Perhaps that's why she sounded so far away.

'After I see Mrs. Castell,' she said firmly. 'If she's awake enough to telephone me, she's awake enough to talk.'

She set off down the little path. Burgess stepped ahead of her and opened the gate.

'She phoned you?' he said casually.

'Yes, just now. Did you see Cal on your way down?'

'I think I saw him distantly along the shore.'

They walked together side by side across the grass. The weather looked as if it was breaking up. Fistfuls of cloud were being hurled high up through the blue sky above them by a stiff breeze which drifted Emily's long yellow hair like a net over her face. And the sky across the other side of the Solway was already solid grey, the line of land practically invisible.

'It's raining in Scotland,' she said.

Burgess was looking thoughtful. Now he stopped and slapped his pocket.

'Damn,' he said. 'I knew there was something. I left my lighter and fags on the floor beside your couch. I'll just pop back and get them.'

He turned on his heel and set off back towards the cottage.

'Hey!' shouted Emily.

'Yes?' He paused and glanced back.

'The key.' She held up her key-ring and shook it so that her keys tinkled together like a cattle-bell. 'Or are you an expert burglar?'

'Thanks,' he said, moving back to her.

She lobbed the keys gently to him. He took them one-handed low down by his left ankle, and set off back to the cottage once more.

Emily resumed her stroll along the grass fronting on to the shore. She was on the look-out for Cal and soon spotted him playing tag with the breakers which the wind was driving in onto the beach. At first he did not hear her call above the crash of the waters, but when she shouted his name a second time he scrambled from the water and came bounding across the sand and stones towards her.

Kneeling down after she had resisted his initial onslaught, she held him at arm's length and examined his eyes and his leg critically.

'You'll do,' she said finally. 'But you're soaking wet again. And it's not a good drying day. This wind could give you rheumatics. Well, if you're very good and walk quietly along with me, I might just be persuaded to buy you a tot of rum.'

Cal barked joyously as if he recognised the word. Other spirits and wine he did not care for in the least. Beer he would lap up if he were thirsty and there was no water. But rum was his heart's ease and delight. Aromatic, black, Jamaica rum. White rums he treated with contempt, like a man who has asked for champagne and is given perry.

106

They had almost reached the hotel before Burgess caught up with them. Emily had shivered slightly as she passed the spot at the bottom of the lane where she had been attacked, and Cal too had sniffed around suspiciously, growling in his throat. But apart from a slight flattening of the grass in places there was no sign of the previous night's conflict.

'O.K.?' asked Burgess as he rejoined them.

'Yes, of course. Did you find your lighter?'

'Yes. Yes, I did.'

'Good.'

They went into the hotel together. Emily stopped at the bottom of the stairs. The reception desk was empty.

'I'll see you in the bar, then,' she said. 'I don't know how long I'll be.'

'I'll be surprised if she can see you,' said Burgess again.

'I'll take the chance. Off you go with Mr. Burgess, Cal.'

Emily turned and tried to run lightly up the stairs. But a few steps reminded her she was in no condition for this, so she settled down to a more sedate pace, using the banister for support.

Room 22 was not difficult to find. It was only a few yards from the first-floor landing. And to make matters easier, there was a woman sitting on a hard chair outside the door. She was reading a magazine with hard concentration and did not look up till Emily came to a halt before her.

'Yes?' she said. She was middle-aged, her greying hair pulled back severely from her brow and face. Her wide-set grey eyes stared up at Emily with neither interest nor any real interrogation in them. Emily had never seen her before.

'I want to see Mrs. Castell,' she said, reaching for the door handle.

'She's resting,' said the woman.

Emily turned the handle. The door was locked.

'I think she's expecting me,' she said politely, and tapped gently on the door.

'Mrs. Castell. It's me, Emily Follett. May I come in?'

There was no sound from within.

'She's sleeping,' said the woman.

'Who are you, please?' asked Emily.

'I'm a nurse. My name's Simpson.'

'Well, Miss Simpson. Mrs. Castell telephoned me not very long ago and asked me to call. So I must persist.'

She rapped on the door again, more loudly this time. There was still no sound of movement inside.

'She's under very heavy sedation, Mrs. Follett,' said the nurse.

My, you caught my name quickly, thought Emily.

'I really must ask you not to disturb her,' Miss Simpson went on. 'Are you sure it was Mrs. Castell herself who rang you?'

'Certain.'

'Then she must have done it almost in her sleep. I can't imagine how. Now please go away, I have strict instructions from the doctor that she

108

must not be disturbed.'

Troubled, Emily turned away. It was true, she told herself. Amanda *had* sounded a little strange and distant. But the more she thought of it, the more certain she was that there had been something other than physical fatigue in her voice.

At the bottom of the stairs she paused, contemplating rejoining battle with Nurse Simpson, but uncertain precisely what she would use for weapons. A rather pretty, fresh-faced young girl leaned over the reception counter and smiled at her.

'Can I help?' she asked.

'I don't think so,' said Emily, then changed her mind. 'On the other hand, perhaps you can, Miss . . . ?'

'Pettle,' supplied the girl. The name fitted.

'I'm a friend of Mrs. Castell,' said Emily.

'Oh dear,' said the girl with genuine sympathy in her eyes. 'It's awful, isn't it? We're all really sorry for her. Have you been up to see her?'

'Yes. Yes I have. But she was asleep. Actually she telephoned me about forty-five minutes ago. The call would have to come through here, wouldn't it?'

'Yes. That's right, I remember. I was having my coffee back there.' She jerked her head towards the door which opened from the rear of the reception area. 'I had to come and put the call through.'

'I see. Was Miss Simpson there too . . . ?'

'The nurse? Yes, she was. Why? There's nothing wrong, is there?'

109

'Oh no, of course not. I just wondered if you'd mentioned to anyone that Mrs. Castell had made a call.'

'Oh no!' The girl was very sure. 'Of course not. You've got to know who you're talking to before you say anything about guests.'

'And you don't know Miss Simpson?'

'No. I'd never seen her before this morning.'

Something in her tone indicated an adverse judgment. Emily gave her a friendly grin.

'Mind you,' said Miss Pettle, suddenly confiding, as if she'd decided in favour of Emily's face, 'I can't say I was delighted at the thought of having her around here all day. I was pretty pleased when she set off back upstairs. I wondered if it had been the doctor who called.'

'You mean she had a call too?' Emily was interested again.

'Oh yes. About fifteen minutes later. And she set off upstairs as if she'd left a kettle on.'

'The doctor, you say?'

'Oh no. I don't know. Just a man's voice. I answered at the switchboard and passed it right over to her.'

'Thank you very much, Miss Pettle. You must let me buy you a drink when you're off duty.'

As she walked away from the desk, something made her glance up the stairwell. Standing on the first-floor landing peering down was the blank, set face of Nurse Simpson. She stepped smartly back as Emily looked up, but there was no doubt who it had been.

In the bar Burgess was sitting by himself in the window-seat. Cal was on his haunches at the

110

other side of the room looking soulfully up into the old grizzled face of the only other man in the bar.

'Why, hello, Joe!' said Emily with pleasure, recognising her dominoes mentor of the previous night. 'Spending your ill-gotten gains?'

The old man chortled with delight.

'All four-square and above board, Em, my dear,' he said. 'But I admit I got enough to buy you a drink with. What'll it be?'

'Later, if you don't mind, Joe. This is my round, I promised earlier. Arthur?'

'Thanks. I've deliberately kept away from that hatch in anticipation,' said Burgess, smiling. 'A pint of keg for me, please.'

'And you, Joe.'

'I won't say no. I'll have a bottle of Special in here,' he said, indicating his half-empty pint pot. 'Livens it up. We're still drinking last night's slops!'

He roared with laughter at the Barman's pained expression.

'And Em, lass. You'd better do something about this dog. I don't know what he wants, but he's pining for something.'

'It's a tot of rum he wants,' said Emily.

She ordered it and Cal moved eagerly forward.

'Right. Head back!' she said.

Obediently he tossed his great square head back and opened his jaws wide. Emily tipped the glass over and poured the small quantity of dark red liquid directly into his gullet.

A tremor of pure pleasure ran through the beast's body.

'Well?' said Burgess, as Emily sat down beside him. 'Any luck?'

'No. Not really. She was asleep and there was a kind of female dragon lying across the door.'

Quickly she recounted what had happened upstairs and after.

'What did you expect if you got into the room?' demanded Burgess. 'That she'd be lying there murdered or something?'

'I don't know,' admitted Emily wearily.

'Look, you've had a rough time in the last day or two. It's upset your judgment a bit, that's all.'

His voice sounded very strong, very certain, very reliable. His face as he looked at her was full of reassurance and care.

She put her hand out and touched his arm.

'You're probably right, Arthur. This place hasn't done my imagination much good, I must admit. I'll be glad to get away.'

He started slightly, surprise showing now.

'Away? I thought you were here for another week at least?'

'No. I've had enough. I'm off tomorrow.'

'But where to? Where will you go?'

'Don't worry! I've got friends around. I'll find somewhere.'

She was touched by the strength of his concern, though not yet certain if she wanted to tap the emotion which must lie behind it.

'You've got friends here too, Emily,' he said earnestly. 'You needn't go off looking for them.'

There was a sentimental note about this which rang false. Emily suddenly found herself no longer touched, but on the edge of irritation.

'No,' she said. 'I've made my mind up. It's me for the road tomorrow.'

'The road?'

'In my car. Along the road. That's what roads are for,' she said with deliberate slowness, as though to a stupid child.

'I didn't know you had a car?'

'Did you think that white Triumph outside the back door belonged to Mrs. Herbert?'

'No. Of course not. I didn't give it a thought. The only time I've been near your back door, I was too concerned about you to notice cars.'

She flushed at the hint of reproach in his voice. He stood up. He hadn't finished his beer.

'Will I see you again before you go?'

'I don't know.'

'No,' he said.

He visibly hesitated, as if pondering something in his mind. Finally he decided. She could almost see the cog wheels turning in his open face.

'Look,' he said. 'Have dinner with me again tonight. That way I can at least make sure you get back to the cottage safely.'

Now she was feeling guilty again. And in any case she'd need something to occupy her this evening if she wasn't to end up sitting in the cottage listening to creakings in the walls. It looked as if some nasty weather was blowing up, which would mean rain beating against window-panes, wind whistling down the chimney. Comforting sounds to those in comfort, with friends, or at home reading some old favourite book in front of a huge fire. But containing little

113

comfortable when backed by the breaking of grey breakers on a stone beach and the forlorn cry of a gull.

'All right,' she said.

'Good!' He smiled his pleasure. But again she sensed something else behind it. A worry. A qualification.

He went on: 'And this time I will call for you, no matter what you say!'

'All right,' she said again.

'I must go now,' he said. 'Thanks for the drink. 'Bye, Cal.' He nodded to old Joe and left.

Emily sipped her drink and scratched Cal's ears thoughtfully.

Joe, who had been listening openly to the conversation, leaned over and said in reproving tones, 'You won't be playing dominoes tonight.'

Again the implication that she would be missed both touched and irritated Emily at the same time.

'No. I'm sorry. But, anyway, you should have Mr. Scott back with you tonight.'

'Michael. Oh, aye.' Joe laughed. 'He plays a nice game, but he's not as pretty as you.'

'How long have you known him?' Emily asked on impulse.

'Not all that long,' said Joe. 'Nine months. A year. Something like that.'

'He's not a local, then? He seems to know his way around.'

'Oh aye. He does that. I think he comes from these parts somewhere, and he gets around everywhere on that great black horse of his. But he's never said much about his background and

114

such. Not that we haven't asked him, mind. We're not backward about being forward up here!'

Emily grinned, remembering the searching inquisition she herself had had to withstand the night before.

'He's at the college, isn't he?'

'That's right.'

'What does he do there? What does *anyone* do there?'

Joe finished his drink and stood up. He looked at Emily, his blue eyes twinkling shrewdly in his weather-lined old face.

'Why don't you ask Michael when you see him? You'll be having a word before you leave?'

Emily wasn't sure whether the second question referred specifically to Michael or just to Joe and his cronies.

'I'll try,' she said, compromising. 'Bye, Joe.'

'Cheerio, lass.'

Cal barked a goodbye as the door closed, and barked even louder a couple of minutes later as it opened again to reveal Michael Scott.

He stood in the doorway, darkly handsome, something between a sneer and a smile on his lips, his aquiline nose with nostrils flared. He was dressed as usual all in black. One hand was on his hip, the other buried deep in the fur of the cat, Miranda, who was draped negligently over his right shoulder.

'Bravo,' said Emily. 'You really must let me take a picture, Mr. Scott. Else my friends won't believe me.'

He didn't ask, believe what? and lay himself

115

open to the insult she was prepared to follow up with. Instead, infuriatingly, he addressed her as though she had not spoken.

'Joe says you're leaving.'

He said it flatly, not as a question. But she answered anyway.

'That's right.'

'When?'

'Tomorrow.'

'Oh.'

He nodded twice as if to some private thought of his own.

Not another fan! thought Emily. Everyone seems to be so unhappy I'm leaving. Perhaps it means there'll be no one left to punch around and generally terrorise!

'Disappointed, Mr. Scott?' she asked coyly.

'A little,' he said. 'I'd hoped you might go today.'

For a second she thought it was a mere gratuitous insult and angrily decided to ignore it. Then looking at the man's face she suddenly realised he meant it. Her anger went.

'Why do you say that, Mr. Scott?' she asked quietly.

'You'll be safer.'

'I'm grateful for your solicitude,' she began with cumbersome irony, but he interrupted her.

'Don't be. I don't take account of personalities. The innocent, the unwary, and the idiot need protecting. I do what I can where I can. How's the leg, old boy?'

Cal, who had been regarding the almost motionless furry shape on Scott's shoulder with considerable suspicion, now offered his leg for inspection from a safe distance.

'Which category do you put me in?' asked Emily, her voice unsteady with some emotion more subtle than anger.

'The same as your dog. The sooner you both get away from here, the better.'

'Just what are you trying to say, Mr. Scott? Or are you merely getting your hand in at oracular utterances? Perhaps you really believe you are *the* Michael Scot.'

'I'm the only one I know. If you're referring to my illustrious medieval ancestor, I agree; we have a lot in common. You could too.'

'What do you mean?'

'You could be dead. Soon. Your own name doesn't seem to be the talisman I'd have thought. Which just goes to show, what's in a name? Have a nice trip tomorrow.'

He was gone before the explosion of wrath whose short fuse he had lit in Emily's mouth could take place.

'Damn you for a stupid, opinionated, narcissistic, perverted . . . ' The fuse fizzled out and Emily decided the only thing to do was have another drink.

Behind the bar putting some money in the till she saw Miss Pettle, the pretty young receptionist.

'Hello there,' she said.

'Oh, hello again.' The girl smiled agreeably.

'Are you free now?'

'Nearly. It's just coming up to my lunch hour.'

'What about that drink, then?'

It would be nice to talk to someone young, happy and uncomplicated, thought Emily.

'Thanks very much. I'd love it. I'll come round when I'm finished here. In fact I'll act as barmaid and then come round and drink it!'

She quickly dispensed the two drinks that Emily ordered, dropped the money in the till and came round from behind the bar.

They drank together.

'Whereabouts are you staying?' asked Miss Pettle.

'Down on the seafront,' said Emily.

'I thought you must be. I noticed you the other night with Mr. Burgess and I knew you weren't booked in here. Did you know him before?'

'No,' said Emily with a smile at finding a youthful equivalent of old Joe's curiosity. 'We just met that day. We were both alone, so it seemed nice to have dinner together. I expect he was pleased to find someone to take the place of his friends. It would have been someone else if it hadn't been me.'

Why am I bothering to dismiss Arthur so lightly for this youngster's benefit? Emily asked herself.

'His friends?' queried Miss Pettle. 'I don't follow.'

God! she scents a true-love magazine-type romance, sighed Emily inwardly.

'I mean the people he should have been here with. The ones who had to cancel,' she explained patiently.

'Oh no,' said Miss Pettle firmly. 'You must be mistaken.'

'Must I? Why?' Emily was still at the stage of being amused.

'Because I took Mr. Burgess's booking myself. By telephone. Just for one. There were no cancellations.'

'Are you sure?' asked Emily, puzzled. 'I'm sure he said . . . '

'Absolutely sure,' affirmed Miss Pettle. 'Would you like me to check?'

'No, don't bother,' said Emily. 'No. On second thought, I would, if you don't mind and it's not too much trouble.'

'No trouble,' grinned the girl. 'I'll do it now. Won't be a sec.'

She plainly scented a mystery now, which was obviously even better than a romance. Everyone had romances, but mysteries were the preserve of the few.

She's welcome to mine, thought Emily.

'I'm right,' said Miss Pettle on her return. 'Booked by phone the morning of the 19th. Arrived that afternoon. He was lucky to get in. Room 32 next to the noisy geyser. We always keep that to last. No other bookings. No cancellations.'

'Thank you very much, Miss Pettle,' said Emily slowly. 'Let me buy you another drink.'

But her thoughts were racing madly away to unimaginable horizons, but always returning to the single plain fact that Arthur Burgess had lied to her and had arrived in Skinburness on the selfsame day that she had taken up residence in Solway Cottage.

119

6

Emily spent the afternoon sitting on the foreshore watching a couple of fishermen. She was perched on the ruins of an old tree trunk and for a while she toyed with imagining that it might have been uprooted from the great forest which legend had it was buried fathoms deep out from Beckfoot. But even broad daylight did not make this reminder of her own brush with Solway mythology in the forms of green men any less disturbing. In any case, daylight was not so broad now. High up the sky was a solid fell of dark grey cloud and much lower a ragged streamer of black was being blown diagonally across the Firth. Criffel had long disappeared and the fishermen leaned into the wind as they tried in vain to get a decent length of cast.

It was a good atmosphere for brooding on things that moved and had their being outside the normal schemes of nature. But Emily's thoughts for the most part were concerned with the wide range of personal problems which troubled her and which sunshine and fair weather could not have changed. Perhaps they might have kept the self-pity at bay.

Suppose, she asked herself, suppose I had to go now to one person whom I could trust and call friend without reservation, just one person in the world, where would I go?

Cal, who had been lying at her feet watching

120

her unblinkingly through his good eye, yawned modestly. Emily laughed and this did her some good.

'I accept your offer,' she said. 'Perhaps if I kiss you, you'll turn into a one-eyed prince.'

Cal rose and lumbered away towards the water.

'All right,' she said. 'Who wants a one-eyed prince, anyway?'

'Who indeed?' said a familiar voice behind her. She started in surprise and turned quickly. The round jolly face of Mr. Plowman peered down at her. He carried a trenching tool over his shoulder and slung round the handle so that it hung down his back like a small haversack.

'Did I startle you? I am sorry,' he said, his smile turning to a look of concern. 'Your nerves have been troubled enough.'

'What do you mean?' asked Emily.

'I'm sorry. I don't mean to pry. But I heard about last night. It was a terrible thing, terrible. Who would want to do a thing like that? I asked Mr. Inwit.'

'Where is Mr. Inwit today?' she asked.

'Resting,' said Plowman solemnly. 'He overdid it yesterday. I rather left him to do it all himself, you remember. He strained his shoulder, I think. So I told him to take a rest, begin the work of tabulating our findings.'

'And what have you found?'

'Sadly very little. My fault again I fear. I'm too haphazard. Dig a trench here, sink a shaft there. It's hit-and-miss stuff, I'm afraid. And we seem to be missing. Today I thought might be the day.

121

But no. And when I saw the weather closing in, I thought, enough's enough. Going back empty-handed is one thing. Going back wet-footed is quite another. How long are you staying, Mrs. Follett?'

'Just till tomorrow,' replied Emily, startled by the suddenness of the question.

'Tomorrow. Fine, fine. We shall miss you, I'm sure, but you're right, you're right. This is no place for the young and beautiful. I firmly believe there are some places where the past clings much more tenaciously to the present than elsewhere, and this is one. And the past feeds on youth and beauty. I'm safe! Oh yes, I'm safe. And Inwit, why, he's even safer. But it's no place for you, my dear. Goodbye. I hope we may meet again; in one of *your* places, perhaps, where *I* shall be at peril!'

Chortling to himself, he went off, his short legs moving him with surprising speed over the tummocks of sea-grass.

Another glad to see me go! thought Emily. That's one thing about Arthur. He at least seemed to be sorry I was leaving.

Still brooding on Plowman's obscure warning, she herself rose now. There was a thin flurry of rain, over in a moment, but threatening worse to come, and she had no desire to get caught in it.

'Come on, Cal!' she called.

She had decided to take the car into Silloth to fill up with petrol and have her oil, tyres, water and the rest checked preparatory to her journey the following day. The car had been standing in the open unused for the past three days and she knew from past experience that this could bring on a fit of temperament.

Sitting in the driver's seat twenty minutes later she was glad of her foresight. Turning the starter key produced no result whatsoever, not even the old dying rattle which was the familiar symptom at such times. She tried again, twice, but still absolutely nothing.

Half angry, half self-congratulatory, she finally climbed out and lifted the bonnet. The limit of her expertise on these occasions was to clean and dry out the plugs, but as this generally proved effective, she felt she was mechanically reasonably competent.

One look at the sight that met her under the bonnet was enough to tell her that this time the limits of her competence were long, long past. Everything that could be loosened was loosened. Everything that could be bent was bent. The fan belt had been cut in half and hung loosely over the twisted distributor. The casing on the plugs was cracked almost to powder. The radiator hose was oozing water in a dozen places.

'Damn, damn, damn, damn!' said Emily, her anger relatively subdued under a wave of sheer amazement. And some little way behind this, still faint but clearly recognisable, came a crest of fear.

Why? she asked herself. Why?

Not why? she answered. Leave 'why?' Let's concentrate on who? Someone who did not want her to leave, obviously. That narrowed things down a lot. In fact there was only one person who had not been openly enthusiastic about her departure. Burgess. As she phoned the garage, the name kept on running round and round in her head, never quite resolving itself into a recognisable figure.

It was me who approached him first, she told herself.

But he certainly didn't want me to leave.

He's taking me out to dinner tonight.

I told him about the car at lunchtime.

Perhaps he is madly in love.

Perhaps he is mad.

If there's one thing that's certain, she told herself finally, it's that I cannot sit at a dinner table with him tonight wondering if he wrecked my car. Asking him direct is out of the question. I've already asked him one very odd question today. But there is something odd about him. Perhaps it's me, I don't know. But I must try to find out.

The outline of a plan began to form in her mind.

The mechanic sent by the garage whistled when he looked under the bonnet.

'It's a mess,' he said.

'How long will it take?'

'All tomorrow certainly, I should think. We'll ring you.'

'I'll ring you,' said Emily firmly.

The mechanic grinned. 'You do that. Every hour on the hour. It'll still take a lot of work. You told the police?'

'I'll deal with it,' said Emily.

'Some yobbo,' said the man. 'Envy, that's usually the reason. Buy yourself an old banger.

They'll never touch it.'

Right, thought Emily grimly. Even if it's not ready till midnight, the minute it is, I'm off out of here. I've waited long enough. But first, Mr. Burgess, let's see what makes you tick.

She assumed Burgess would come for her at seven. To be quite safe she set off at six and positioned herself behind the hedge at the bottom of the lane, close to where she had been attacked the night before. The memory of that adventure had almost faded alongside this new excitement and the pain in her stomach muscles was now just an ignorable ache.

Cal she had reluctantly left behind. He was too lively and too bulky for the cloak-and-dagger stuff.

Burgess came early, just after half past six, and she was glad of her own foresight. She let him get about fifteen yards towards the cottage, then slipped out of concealment and hurried round the corner, up the lane.

Miss Pettle was back behind the reception desk. She looked up as Emily approached and was obviously eager to talk. But Emily forestalled her.

'Could I have Mr. Burgess's key?' she said lightly. 'I have to get something from his room.'

Miss Pettle's eyes lit up. Mystery and/or romance was again in the air. She lifted key number 32 from its place on the board, but did not hand it over immediately.

'Shall I come with you?' she said.

'Oh, don't bother,' said Emily. 'I won't be a second.'

She leaned over the counter and tweaked the key from the girl's hand.

'Thanks,' she said, and trotted rapidly up the stairs.

The room was on the second floor. On the first-floor landing she noticed that Miss Simpson seemed to have abandoned her post outside Amanda's room. For a second she hesitated, then made up her mind and carried on up the next flight.

Room 32 was right at the end of a corridor. As she reached it she thought she heard a door open and close behind her, but when she turned there was no one there. She had foreseen a crisis of conscience at this point, or at least of courage. Now she marvelled at the easy speed with which she turned the key in the lock and slipped into the room.

Now, she realised, came the real crisis. What on earth was she looking for?

'I'll know it when I see it,' she told herself firmly, echoing words she recalled hearing her mother use when asked for a description of a lost umbrella at a police station. The memory ridiculously brought sudden tears to her eyes.

Fiercely she started pulling open drawers in the tallboy which occupied half a wall. Socks, handkerchiefs, underclothing. In the wardrobe, shirts, suits. He did himself quite nicely thank you. It was all fifty-guinea stuff and she recognised the name of the tailors. She had once gone there with Sterne.

A couple of suitcases, matching, calf-skin. Empty.

A pair of very sexy red silk pyjamas under the coverlet. *Martin Chuzzlewit* (leather bound, one of a very expensive set) on the bedside table. She smiled. That fitted him somehow. She suddenly felt oddly affectionate towards Burgess.

Perhaps it was the red pyjamas.

Now she was beginning to experience the crisis of conscience. And of courage.

Brightly she whistled a couple of notes of 'Whenever I Feel Afraid'. And let out a bitten-off scream as the tune seemed to be taken up by some monstrous bubbly tuba whose notes reverberated all around her. It took her half a minute to identify the source of the noise as the troublesome geyser which made the room so undesirable.

Shakily she sat down on the edge of the bed and tried to manage a laugh.

'I see what you mean, Miss Pettle,' she said. 'And Arthur, if there is anything odd about you, which I begin to doubt, you can't be blamed. Not with *that* next door!'

She glanced at her watch. It was time to go. She automatically adjusted her hair in the dressing-table mirror before her. It was a simple table with only two small side-drawers. She opened the right hand one. Cuff-links, diamond solitaire.

He did himself very well for a personnel officer.

In the left-hand drawer was a little address book.

She thumbed through it rapidly. There weren't

many names in it and none of them meant anything to her.

In the last few pages were some telephone numbers without names.

She had closed the book and was putting it back in the drawer when something she had seen completed the slow journey from the sighting part of her brain to the sorting area. Slowly she sank back down on to the bed and opened the book again. It only took her a moment to find it.

Two telephone numbers bracketed together, one London, one a local Silloth number. The local number meant nothing at all to her, but the London number did.

It belonged to her past, present, but she hoped not future, husband, Sterne Follett.

The geyser bubbled again, Wagnerian in style now. But even without its covering concert it was doubtful whether she would have heard the bedroom door open.

And even the voice which spoke now lacked the power to startle her, so deeply lost in a maze of thought and memory she was.

'We must have missed each other in the lane, Emily. It was thoughtful of you to come up here.'

She turned to look at Burgess. For a moment she thought he was going to pretend that nothing odd had taken place. But the twisted grin on his face underlined the gentle irony of his words. In any case, she was in no mood for pretence.

Holding the book out to him she said, 'What's your connection with my husband, Arthur?'

Gently he closed the door behind him and

almost as an afterthought turned the key in the lock.

'It's quite simple really, Emily,' he said. 'Sterne's my employer. Not that I'd dare call him Sterne to his face. Mr. Follett, sir. I work for him.'

'In what capacity?'

He shrugged. 'I don't have an official title. Mr. Follett doesn't believe in labelling his personal staff. Flexibility is all important. It's only degrees of efficiency that interest Mr. Follett.'

His voice changed, became soft, reasonable, beautifully modulated.

Closing her eyes, Emily recognised the parody of Sterne being dogmatic. If any doubts had remained, this would have convinced her that Burgess knew her husband.

'I'm an agent, really. I represent Mr. Follett's interests in whatever capacity he thinks suitable.'

'And in this case?'

'I suppose you would call me a kind of spy.'

Burgess spoke quite unemotionally. Emily opened her eyes in surprise at hearing the word she was planning to use in a minor role somewhere in the great outburst of abuse she felt building itself up in her. Not that it mattered. There were plenty of other words.

'How long have you been spying on me?'

'Me personally? Oh, just since you came to Cumberland. But before that there was someone else. Your every move since you left him will have been closely charted.'

Emily thought carefully. 'You got here the same day as I did?'

129

'Yes. Orders arrived. Drop everything. Go to Skinburness and spy.'

'It was you who searched the cottage.'

'Guilty again, I'm afraid. I thought I'd done a good job there. You were sharp to spot it.'

'What were you looking for?'

'Something Mr. Follett seemed to think you might have. A piece of communal property perhaps?'

Emily didn't pursue this. Another thought had come into her mind.

'Was it you later as well?'

'Oh no,' Burgess demurred, 'I'm not your green man. If he's on the payroll I haven't been told.'

'How much were you told?'

'Next to nothing. Just to keep an eye on you and report what you were up to. Mention anything out of the ordinary. You know the kind of thing.'

'No. I can't say I do. What about getting to know me? Having dinner?'

Burgess shrugged and a shadow of what might have been pain passed over his face.

'No. That was my idea. Spur of the moment stuff when you started to talk to me on the beach.'

'Initiative. Was it commended? Did you get a bonus, a mention in despatches?' Emily's voice took on an ugly jeering note.

'No,' said Burgess quietly. 'I was told it must stop.'

'Stop?'

'That any further attempt on my part to get to

know you better would be frowned on.'

'So you stopped. That explains your blow hot, blow cold act. But then you started again.'

'That was after you were hurt.'

'I see. Orders again.' The sneer was back. Burgess did not reply. He had remained standing by the door during all the conversation. Only his lips moved.

'You did my car too?'

'I'm sorry about that. I had to. You were so uncertain at lunchtime that it seemed possible you might just take off into the blue on an impulse. I couldn't let that happen.'

'You mean your efficiency rating might suffer? You were scared to lose me?'

'Yes,' he said, so quietly now she could hardly hear him. 'I was scared to lose you.'

His tone of voice made her pause for a moment, but only for a moment. There was too much anger inside her to be turned aside by a whole regiment of soft words.

She returned to the attack.

'You said you report. Tell me, how do you get back to your master with your assorted tittle-tattle.'

'I telephone.'

'Where?'

'The first of those numbers till a couple of days ago. Then I was instructed to phone the other.'

Now she did pause for a long time, sudden interest and something like apprehension filling her mind as she stared down at the numbers. The London one she could understand. But the local one . . . If Sterne should be near . . .

'When did you last phone in?'

'This morning,' he said. 'From the cottage when I went back for my lighter.'

Emily's mind was racing. Burgess phones Sterne. Someone phones Nurse Simpson, who takes up sentry duty outside Amanda's door. Connection?

She stood up and faced him.

'Open the door,' she said.

'Emily, listen,' he said, some emotion breaking the monotone of his voice for the first time.

'The door,' she said.

'Listen, please. I was warned off seeing too much of you, but it didn't make any difference. I was coming to your cottage last night when I found you in the lane. Please believe me. I shouldn't be having dinner with you tonight. He won't like it!'

His voice rose to a near-shout. He reached out a hand towards her. She stared at him with contempt.

'You poor miserable creature! You'd better report what I've been doing for the past half-hour. Perhaps he'll be in a forgiving mood and wipe away your tears. Now open the door or I scream till someone opens it for me.'

Silently he turned and unlocked the door. She didn't look at him as she left. Downstairs she ignored with equal indifference old Joe's cheery 'Good evening' and Miss Pettle's inquisitive smile.

There was a phone booth opposite the cocktail-bar door. She stepped inside, and firmly, calmly, dialled the local number she had read in Burgess's book. The book itself she had let fall on the bedroom floor, but the number was printed deep in her mind.

Distantly she heard the usual clickings which precede connection. Then the ringing tone began. It sounded twice before the phone was answered.

'Who is that speaking?' Emily drew in a sharp breath as she heard the cold, impersonal tones of the man at the other end of the line. She had been prepared to hear Sterne. But this was not Sterne.

'Who is that speaking?' the voice repeated. Emily replaced the receiver.

It was a voice she had heard before. Once. But what on earth could the connection be between Sterne Follett and the college?

Puzzled, no, more than puzzled, deeply worried she stepped out of the booth and stood uncertain what to do next. Someone came out of the cocktail bar, releasing a brief gust of chatter, glass-clinking and music. It was only a couple of yards away but suddenly it seemed like an infinitely desirable world she could never re-enter.

So deeply plunged in her own concern was she that it was only the second hoarsely called 'Mrs. Follett!' that penetrated her mind. Later it would have been nice to say that all personal worries fled from her mind at the sight of Amanda Castell, haggard, hair falling at will over her face, wearing a blue gingham night-dress, leaning on the banister rail of the stairway as though

133

nothing else in the world was holding her up. But the cry that rose in Emily's mind was a resentful 'I've got troubles of my own!'

She couldn't speak the words, however, any more than she could have taken another step towards the door.

'Please, Mrs. Follett,' said Amanda, her big face aquiver with urgency. She did try another step and nearly stumbled headlong down the stairs.

Miss Pettle craned her neck over the reception desk and was watching the old woman — for now she looked a good sixty — with deep concern. Behind her on the stairs appeared Burgess and with him round, little Plowman.

'Mrs. Castell!' said the latter in a voice of deep concern, and they both hurried forward to support her. The American woman looked round at the words and then turned back to Emily, an expression of such panic on her face that Emily's state of near-trance was at last broken and she could rush forward.

Weeping, the older woman collapsed into her arms and Emily found she needed the help of the two men to support her considerable weight.

'Come along, come along now, Mrs. Castell. There, there. It'll all be all right. You'll see.'

Clucking and cooing, Plowman supervised the return of Amanda to her room. All strength seemed to have left her limbs now and her head rolled grotesquely from side to side as if she lacked the power to hold it still. Tears stained her face, but she was no longer sobbing, and Emily gently wiped away those that remained when they finally managed to get her back into bed.

She lay still, exactly as they had arranged her, her head fallen sideways on the pillow, her mouth funnelled wide open, her eyes closed. As she looked at her, Emily recalled vividly being taken to see an aged aunt of her father's who had just suffered a stroke and her own horror at seeing the once lively and kindly face so helpless and hollow on the pillow.

Plowman stared down at the woman for a moment.

'She looks far gone,' he said. 'We must get the doctor back. And where on earth has that nurse got to? This is really outrageous.'

Indignation stamped all over his chubby face, he bustled out of the room.

'What do you think?' said Emily to Burgess, their quarrel forgotten in the face of this tragedy.

Burgess shrugged. 'She's been through a lot. If her heart was bad . . . and it's had a lot of work to do with that weight. I'll see what Plowman's up to.'

Abruptly he broke off and turned and left the room. Emily watched him go, surprised at the concern he seemed to be feeling.

A rough diamond with a heart of gold, she thought ironically. But all humour fled as she turned back to the sick woman and bent over her to listen, suddenly fearful that she had stopped breathing.

'Bloody nerve,' said Amanda. 'What's he mean, that weight? I've got big bones. No, don't look surprised, hon, and just stay there between me and the door.'

'Amanda!' said Emily. 'But what . . . why . . . I thought you were dead.'

'Yeah? Well, I don't know, I guess I might as well be. Listen, hon, and listen good. I don't know how deep you're in this, but in it you are. With a name like yours you must be.'

She laughed shortly.

'I'm breaking all the rules, aren't I? For all I know you're laughing like a drain up your sleeve. Hey, listen to me! Fen would have fallen over himself laughing at that.'

A shadow crossed her face.

'I'm not laughing,' said Emily quietly. 'Not up my sleeve or anywhere.'

'No,' said the old woman, looking at her shrewdly. 'I reckon you're not. Listen, hon, I just want to know one thing, just a straight yes or no. O.K.?'

'If I can,' said Emily. 'Of course.'

'Right. Is my Fen still alive? That's it. You must have guessed. Well?'

Emily looked helplessly down at the anxious face beneath her, the lines of worry deep along the brow, the muscles tautened against the feared reply. The thought flashed across her mind that had she been as certain now that Amanda was dying as she was only a few moments earlier she would have told the comforting lie. But there were reserves of strength here which seemed good for another quarter century.

'I don't know,' she said. 'Please believe me, I honestly don't know.'

Amanda's hand tightened over her wrist as though she meant to squeeze the truth out by

136

main force, but the pressure relaxed almost instantly.

'Yeah. O.K. I believe you,' she said hopelessly.

'What's this all about, Mandy?' asked Emily, using the American's pet name for the first time.

'You don't know, huh? Can you find out? Please, hon. I'm too old . . . Listen, they're coming back. Don't let him know you've been talking to me for your own sake, huh?'

Her mouth gaped wide, her head fell slackly across the pillow and she began breathing hoarsely.

'Which 'him'? whispered Emily anxiously, but she did not know if Amanda even heard her question as the door opened behind her.

It was Rogers, the doctor who had attended her own injuries after the attack. He raised his eyebrows in surprise at the sight of her and her stomach muscles ached in response.

But he went straight over to Amanda without a word and began to take her pulse.

Emily moved to the door.

'Mrs. Follett,' said the doctor. 'Perhaps you could spare a moment. There is another room, I believe.'

He glanced at a second door in the wall behind him.

'Certainly, Doctor,' said Emily, and went through into a pleasantly furnished sitting room. It was on a corner of the building and while the bedroom window just overlooked the road which wound eastwards over the marsh, this room had two windows one of which gave a long long view out over the Grune to the sea. The threatened rain had still not got much further than the occasional violent flurry, but visibility was very bad and the long, light evenings that had stretched deep into the past few nights seemed distant memories. It might have been November.

There was no sign of life between the garden below and the ridge of grass and gorse which rose up to hide the shore. Only the square bulk of the college rose at a distance of about half a mile and as usual, neither light nor movement indicated the presence of human occupation there.

'How are you feeling now, Mrs. Follett?' asked the doctor, who had come in unheard behind her. Again her stomach ached at the reminder.

'Well enough,' she said.

'I'm glad you're here,' he went on. 'What happened to Mrs. Castell?'

'I don't know,' said Emily. 'Why? Is she all right?'

'Yes, I think so. She looks worse than she is, I think,' he replied, looking at her with just a hint of enquiry in his eyes. 'I've given her an injection to put her to sleep.'

So the poor old girl didn't admit she was conscious, thought Emily.

'Good. Perhaps she just woke up and was a bit dazed, so set off to look for the nurse, or something,' suggested Emily. 'Where *is* the nurse, anyway?'

'I don't know,' said the doctor grimly, 'but I'll have words to say to her when I find out.'

'It's a strange way to behave,' agreed Emily. 'Do you know her well?'

'Why, no. I've never used her before. I shall be reluctant to again, even though it was a favour.'

'A favour?'

'That's right,' said Rogers. 'I borrowed her from the college. The old lady needed someone, there was no one locally available that I knew, then someone suggested the college. Presumably they have a medical room and presumably the middle of the summer is a quiet time for them. Hence Nurse Simpson.'

He hesitated, then seemed to make up his mind.

'Mrs. Follett,' he said. 'What's all this about?'

'What do you mean, Doctor?'

He shrugged.

'You tell me. Everyone's acting just a bit oddly. And Mrs. Castell . . . '

'Yes?'

'She's said one or two things under sedation. Odd things. She doesn't seem to think her husband's dead. Or at least not drowned. And this seems to be connected with something she ought to do.'

'She's had a nasty shock,' Emily said.

'Yes. She has,' he said slowly. 'But I'm not absolutely sure what it was.'

He glanced at his watch.

'Good Lord. Must be off or my dinner will be cold,' he said with professional callousness. He ushered Emily into the corridor and himself took a last peep at Amanda before joining her.

'Sleeping like a baby,' he said with satisfaction. 'I'll get Roberts to tell one of the maids to keep an eye on her, but she shouldn't move till morning. Meanwhile I'll try to track down the absent Nurse Simpson.'

Ahead of them in the corridor an old maid (in every sense of the phrase, Emily suspected) had been moving from room to room. Emily had watched her as she waited for the doctor, thinking she was doubtless turning down the beds while the guests were at dinner. This had reminded her of her own former commitment to dine with Burgess and she suddenly felt hungry.

As they passed the maid standing outside another door, Emily paused. 'Don't bother with number 22,' she said. 'Mrs. Castell is sleeping.'

'Right, ma'am,' said the woman, gave a perfunctory knock at the door in front of her, and entered.

'Oh,' she said, stopping dead. 'Sorry, sir.'

Emily glanced casually through the door as she moved away, and found herself looking at the weedy frame of Inwit, stripped to his vest and pants. The maid stepped back, closed the door, and made a wry face at Emily as though inviting her to join in her contempt for the whole male sex. But Emily was quite unable to respond to the invitation. Her mind was buzzing with the swarm of thoughts sent up by the sight of a large dark briuse on Inwit's right shoulder and a thin double scratch down his right cheek.

7

The picture remained with her all the way back to the cottage, like an after-image on the retina caused by staring at the sun. But this was more like an after-image of darkness. And overlaid on it as she leaned into the wind blowing off the sea up the lane was the memory of Inwit, a thin line of perspiration on his brow, scraping earth from a large, loosely piled mound back into the trench he and Plowman had dug with such obvious care and effort.

It's absurd, she told herself as she lit the old newspaper which she had hastily bundled up in the fireplace. It had suddenly seemed an absolutely urgent requirement that she should have a fire. Warmth, light. She felt she knew now how the savages who were her ancestors must have looked forward to seeing that yellow flame leaping in the darkening forest glades.

The sticks she had used were slightly damp and sputtered and sparked before they caught, but once they did the handful of coals she had strewn on top quickly took flame and a little comforted she drew her knees up to her chin and stared into the moving glow.

Faces began to form there as they had done when she was a young girl. Her father, dead now for seven years. A school friend not seen for much longer. Burgess, anxious, penitent. Plowman smiling. Inwit pensive. An animal face, unrecognised for a moment, then setting into Miranda, Michael Scott's cat.

Beside her, Cal sniffed and growled as though somehow scenting her thoughts. Emily smiled.

Now Inwit reappeared and the smile died away. Not pensive now, but sneering. Then he too faded with the shifting glow and Sterne looked at her thoughtfully, patiently out of the flames. A coal shifted and the fire caved in in the middle leaving nothing but ash and burning coals.

Quickly she stood up before the spell could be reestablished, picked up her telephone directory and looked for the police number.

Let Parfrey sort it out, she thought as she listened to the ringing tone. Parfrey is paid to investigate suspicions. No matter how stupid or vague. It's his job.

Dring-dring. Dring-dring. After the first half-dozen rings she had known with absolute certainty that no one was going to answer. But she let the noise go on, almost hypnotised by its rhythmicality, for another two or three minutes before replacing the receiver.

There was an alternative number in the book, a Carlisle number, to be used if no reply was obtainable locally. She considered it for a moment, then closed the book. To start at the beginning seemed worse than remaining as she was. And in some unacknowledged control centre of her mind she knew that she had no intention of doing that either.

It took her about thirty minutes to admit this

openly. These she spent exercising Cal up and down the beach immediately in front of the cottage. A wind blew gustily, and its breath was damp. In fine weather there would have been another hour of good daylight ahead, but tonight everything had already taken on the greyness of four o'clock on a December evening. Lights shone palely in windows, leaning on the glass like vinegar for the night was not yet dark enough for the full contrast to show.

Soon it will be too dark, the control centre reminded. It's nearly time.

But first there was something else to do.

It'll keep till later, she told herself. But superstitiously she knew it wouldn't. Despite everything, she couldn't just go the next day. There had been an agreement.

It was rather like making out a will before battle, she decided, as she took out her pen and sat at the rickety little card table with a writing pad laid out before her.

This could be the last letter I ever send to you, she thought as she began to write, at first with meticulous care, 'Dear Sterne.'

Damn him! she suddenly thought. If he wants perfect tidiness let him get his secretary to copy it out! Her writing accelerated.

'I have decided to leave Skinburness tomorrow. I feel that the presence of Arthur Burgess more than compensates for the fact that I haven't been able to perform my part of our bargain.'

She studied what she had written. Did it sound too abrupt? Or too apologetic? Bargain.

That was the word, though Sterne wouldn't like it.

Bargain.

It had seemed suspiciously, incredibly, simple at the time. She should have known. Nothing Sterne was mixed up in was simple.

It had been just over a week before. Yet it seemed very distant. Months, years.

She had left him. Finally. Irrevocably. The effort had left her weak and trembling like a Victorian maid in a decline.

That night Sterne had telephoned the hotel. How he found out where she was he did not say. She had nearly slammed the phone down on its rest, but didn't, fearing this might bring him round in person. At least while he was speaking on the phone she need not fear the knock on the door.

Fear. A strange word to use of your husband. She had remembered then the words he had used when she had told him she wanted a divorce. 'I will never divorce you, though that is not to say that I might not be constrained some day to dispose of you.'

But it had been better then, she thought. No threats. No mockery.

He had sounded as calm and reasonable as ever, much less dangerous and angry than she feared. He had listened in complete silence to the little set-piece she had prepared for just such an occasion. The silence continued when she came to a halt and stretched beyond her speech, around it, wrapping it up and making it seem small, mean, insignificant.

'You should go away,' he said finally.

'Yes, yes. I am,' she answered aggressively.

'Good. Good.' He sounded as if he meant it. 'Where are you going?'

She almost listed the two or three alternatives she had been thinking of, then cut herself short just in time.

'Oh no,' she said, congratulating herself on spotting the trap. 'That's my business from now on.'

'True,' he said. 'True. After the divorce, that is.'

Divorce. After what he'd said before she'd stopped visualising the prospect of the real freedom offered by a divorce. The best she could hope for was some Reno-like trumpery perhaps, if she could afford it. But real, good old English divorce, pronounced in open court by a bewigged judge and reported in the Sunday papers, that she could not hope for, not with Sterne.

'Yes. After the divorce,' he repeated.

'What do you mean?' she asked, unable to keep the suspicion and disbelief out of her voice.

'You must have your holiday,' he said gently. 'Think things out. If you are still resolved, we must each seek our freedom.'

'Yes,' she said uneasily. 'I will.'

She knew there had to be more to come.

'It occurs to me you might perhaps combine business with pleasure, a bit of my business with your pleasure, I mean,' he said musingly. 'You might be able to do me a small service during your holiday.'

'Which is?'

'Do you remember mentioning to me a place called Skinburness? On the Solway Firth? I believe you went there as a child. Would that be the kind of place you envisaged for your holiday?'

It wasn't. It was just the opposite of what she had in mind. But strangely the second Sterne mentioned the place, her childhood memories returned and it seemed infinitely attractive and desirable.

'It might be,' she answered guardedly, keeping this emotion out of her voice.

'If it were, by any chance, you might be able to help me in a business matter in which some small degree of discretion is needed.'

'What would I have to do?'

'Nothing positive, my dear. Just accept delivery of a packet. It will have a book in it. You needn't open it, just accept it, if it's given to you or left with you. And then give it in turn to me.'

'What's this all about, Sterne? Why not use the post?'

'The safety factor, my dear. And time. If you did receive it, I'd expect you to break your holiday short and bring it down to our home straight away.'

There was a faint underlining of 'our.'

'Let me get this straight,' said Emily finally. 'Are you saying if I do this you'll give me a divorce?'

The direct question did not seem to disturb Sterne at all.

'I was merely asking a favour of you, dear. I

would trust we are going to remain good friends even after our marriage has ended.'

That had been it. A bargain struck, however vague. Emily knew her husband well enough to believe that an understanding had been reached even if he refused to acknowledge the precise form of words she used.

Two hours later a messenger had delivered a letter to her from Sterne. It told her that Solway Cottage, Skinburness, had been booked in her maiden name for a fortnight in two days' time, and added that during her stay a book might be delivered to her in a brown-paper parcel. If this happened she would oblige her husband by returning to town immediately and delivering it to him personally. He wished her a pleasant and health-giving stay.

What the book might be, Emily had no idea. But if this was the price of divorce it could contain pornographic pictures of the Archbishop of Canterbury for all she cared.

So two days later she pointed the gleaming white nose of her Triumph up the M.I and arrived in Skinburness the same day. Since when the only book that had been delivered to her in any form had been Michael Scott's. And that had not remained with her long.

Her stomach ached at the memory as she scrawled her signature at the bottom of the letter.

To hell with Sterne! What did it matter if they never got divorced? She was not likely to want to marry again in a hurry.

And it was quite imperative that she got out of

this place as soon as possible.

She thought of trying Parfrey again. She thought of just locking every door and window in the place and sitting in front of the fire all night.

Instead she found herself pulling on a warm sweater and zipping up her parka while Cal watched her expectantly. She pulled a woollen ski-hat on to her head, then stood still for a moment. There was something else she needed. In the old-fashioned umbrella rack standing outside the kitchen was a small but extremely sturdy child's spade. As she took it out she dislodged a whole wigwam of old golf-clubs and walking sticks and surprised herself by not starting in the least at the sudden noise. Cal, on the other hand, was very shocked and leapt round teeth bared, mane bristling.

'You're too excitable by half,' said Emily, and at the open door of the cottage she turned, raised her index finger and said firmly, 'Stay!'

Disappointed, the big dog reluctantly stretched himself out over the threshold, though he brightened visibly when Emily added the much more positive command word, 'Guard!'

She was unable to decide exactly why she had not taken him with her, and indeed her conscious mind deliberately shied away from the puzzle. But vague ideas about covering her retreat, and even vaguer ones about having someone to go back to flitted around the back of her mind in a recess even deeper than the control room.

But she was not a woman who could put up

with too much vagueness too long.

As she passed through the broken wire fence which prevented the Philistines from driving their cars along the Grune, she paused and spoke to herself inwardly with great clarity.

Inwit the archaeologist, she said, is possibly the man who attacked me, just about here, last night. I have no way of proving that. Also possibly he has in the company of Plowman buried the body of Fenimore Castell in the middle of a gorse clump. *That* I can prove or disprove. And that is what I am about to do.

Facing facts, she now decided, was not the rapid road to comfort and self-respect her R.I. mistress had so frequently promised.

I must be mad.

It began to rain.

At least the ground will be soft! she giggled to herself. And found her legs had carried her another hundred yards or more without her noticing.

After that it was as easy to go on as to go back.

She recognised the sentiment as being one of the more profound of Macbeth's, a man whom she regarded as the most stupid of all dramatic heroes, with the possible exception of Faustus. The recollection made her pause again.

Visibility was rapidly worsening and she found that in this light, in this atmosphere, bushes really did begin to look like bears. But she knew also that the only thing which could bring her real peace of mind now was for her quest to prove fruitless and Inwit's trench to turn out to be nothing more than a trench. So on she went once more.

When the faint outline of the college showed up through the mirk to her right she slowed down. It was not far past here, she recollected, that she had turned off. Things looked very different now from their appearance in the bright sunshine of midday.

She made several false starts, actually penetrating right to the centre of one clump of gorse and briar before deciding it was the wrong one. Inside there it was fairly sheltered and comparatively dry. Despite the throat-tickling, musty smell of the place she was tempted to rest for a moment with a cigarette. Then something rustled in the grass and startled she hurried away, scratching her hands and face as she forced her way through the clinging briar.

Out in the open again she gulped in huge lungfuls of damp air and after a moment could almost smile at her panic. Almost.

The next path she investigated was the one. She knew it immediately and followed its twists as easily as though it were a pavement she'd walked along a hundred times.

But when she reached the open place where she had encountered the archaeologists she suddenly ceased to be certain. It looked right and felt right. But there were no signs of digging there, no freshly disturbed ground, no piles of earth.

Puzzled, she stooped down and began to feel her way over the grassy turf, already half convinced she was mistaken. But a minute's examination at this level reassured her.

Well now, she thought. What a tidy little man you are, to be sure, Mr. Inwit! Fancy, you've put every one of those sods back just as you took it out. And brushed away any loose dirt left over. It would be almost impossible to tell you'd ever been here.

Swiftly she began to pull the sods up, using her spade for leverage where necessary. In fact the sods had been replaced too recently to have re-bound themselves with the earth beneath, which in any case was soft and loose. She could burrow more swiftly down through it with her hands than with her tiny spade and she knelt astride the trench, scrabbling out the loose earth between her legs like a dog.

It was hard work, none the less, and soon her stomach muscles began to ache abominably. When she had scooped out a hollow of about two feet in depth she took a breather.

I really must be mad, she thought again, wiping a mixture of sweat and rain from her brow with a hand so dirty it all immediately turned to mud.

'Right!' she said out loud. 'Another foot. If he's deeper than that, he can stay there!'

Her frivolity sprang from a conviction that her search was going to be utterly fruitless, that nothing at all was there. A sudden hardening of the earth supported her theory. She must be at the bottom of the freshly dug stratum.

Though, of course, her uncontrollable control room added, if you buried a corpse, you would probably stamp down very hard on the layer of

151

earth immediately above it.

At that moment her fingers touched a piece of glass. Gingerly, worried in case she cut herself, she tried to pull it out of the earth, but it wouldn't come. In any case, her careful probe told her, it didn't seem to have any sharp edges. And it seemed to be perfectly circular in shape.

Her heart lurched.

Praying softly, she moved her index finger slowly along the smooth surface till it reached the edge. Then a little further. A little further.

Gently she bumped into some kind of protuberance.

And knew at once, before the message reached her conscious mind, that it was a human nose.

'Oh God,' she said, her nerveless fingers tracing the outline of this earth-strewn face still invisible at the bottom of the trench. 'Oh God!'

Slowly she rose, slowly turned, but once it was behind her she began to run. The twists and turns of the narrow path were forgotten now. It was only a few yards long, but she seemed to plunge and duck for half a mile through clutching arms of briar and fists of gorse, before she fell almost full length on to the main path and could hear clear once more the swell and pull of the sea.

But there was something else too. A drumming in the earth beneath her shivering body. She looked up. Out of the dark loomed a shape so large that she knew it would fall on her and crush her where she lay.

She screamed.

'Whoa!' cried a man's voice and the shape

reared up over her and instantly became a horse. Large but not monstrous. Almost movingly familiar.

She scrambled to her feet.

'What the hell? You!' said Michael Scott.

'Oh yes,' she said. 'Yes. Please, please . . . '

She was ready to collapse and weep in his arms or round his horse's neck. Anywhere, in fact, but the sympathetic murmurings did not materialise.

'You damned fool!' said Scott. 'I warned you to get away from here.'

'I'm sorry,' she faltered, amazed to hear herself apologising so abjectly, but ready to do anything to retain the pleasure of his company.

'You may be sorrier,' he said savagely. 'Let's get you home before any more harm's done.'

'Oh, it's too late for that, I'm afraid, Mr. Scott. Far too late. The harm's done now!'

The voice was Plowman's. He laughed as he spoke.

What happened next was so rapid that it was only much much later that Emily sorted it out into sequence and scripted it. Total acting time, she decided, was about ten seconds.

She turned at the voice. Behind her, having obviously just come along the path, were two dark shapes she knew at once were Inwit and Plowman. The former carried a trenching tool before him like a short battle-axe. The latter stood like a country gentleman on his estate, all tweedy, with the smooth, dully-shining barrels of a shot-gun resting in the crook of his arm. They both wore knee-length gumboots.

A strong hand seized Emily from behind and dragged her round into the neck of the black horse. Something rose on the saddle in front of Scott and looked at her inquiringly.

It was Miranda.

'Get up!' cried Scott, lifting her bodily one-handed by the neck of her parka and trying to throw her over the horse in front of him.

The shot-gun came smoothly up in Plowman's hands. The horse turned and reared, Emily clung desperately on. Plowman ducked away from the plunging hooves and fired. The horse screamed as pellets scored a bloody line along his neck. Scott gave a low groan, clapped his right hand to his left shoulder and his fingers slowly relaxed their grip on Emily, who was thrown to the ground with Miranda on top of her as the horse reared again and bolted with Scott lying loosely forward in the saddle half over to one side.

The gun came up again, levelled after the rapidly disappearing horse, when a smaller shape just as black detached itself from the ground and launched itself upwards at Plowman's face. It was Miranda. The man screamed as he fell backwards with the cat spitting and clawing at his face. The second barrel went off harmlessly into the air. Inwit, who had moved menacingly towards Emily with his trenching tool at the ready, hesitated, then turned and ran towards his partner.

Something told Emily this might be the last chance she would ever have to make an independent decision. She scrambled to her feet and ran blindly off along the path. Logically she would have preferred to be running back towards the village. But that would have meant running past the archaeologists. So she ran wildly through the rain in the direction of the Point.

Ten seconds, she worked out later. No longer. Ten seconds to send a wounded, perhaps dying man galloping along the shore on a panic-stricken and bleeding horse. Ten seconds to provoke a raging, fearless cat to try to claw your eyes out. (With a bit of luck she might even have succeeded.) Ten seconds to send a terrified helpless woman running into the night in peril of her life.

A good ten seconds' work, Mr. Plowman and Mr. Inwit.

But these thoughts came much later. Now there was only the rain in her face, the wind buffeting her weakening body, the uncertain ground betraying her every step. And, worst of all, the sense of pursuit.

She knew as surely as she had ever known anything that whatever else Inwit and Plowman had to do that night, or any other night, first of all they had to kill her.

She stumbled and fell heavily, her foot twisted in a rabbit hole. She had seen them running over the sand earlier in the week, gambolling in the early-morning sunlight. And she had blessed the animal creation as fervently and unconsciously as the Ancient Mariner.

Now consciously, but just as fervently, she damned them all to hell and gingerly fingered her ankle.

She was lucky. It all seemed in order. She tried

155

it out. There was no pain. So far, so good. This enforced halt could be a blessing in disguise. She crouched nearer to the bushes against which she had fallen; not too near, that might trap her; just near enough for concealment.

Good. She was thinking logically again. She forced into her mind a picture of the Grune. A peninsula about one mile in length and one quarter mile in width bounded by the Solway on one hand and Skinburness Creek on the other . . . The words, she realised with a humourless smile, were none other than Inwit's, spoken to Amanda Castell only two nights before.

Her problem now was to get back to civilisation, people, light, as quickly as possible. The nearest building was the college, but somehow she did not fancy that. It held too many mysteries. The quickest way to the village was to return the way she had come, but she fancied that even less. Inwit and Plowman had seemed faintly comic as archaeologists. As hunters she was ready to treat them with much more respect. Miranda would have only delayed them. She hoped the beast had as much discretion as it had courage and had beaten a retreat when Inwit went to his partner's aid. They didn't look like members of the R.S.P.C.A.

She forced her mind back to the problem in hand. Not backwards; that was out. Alternatives were either to cut across the Grune and make her way back via the fields which lay along the middle of it or to continue forward and follow the path round the Point, along the creek and so back to the hotel. The route was the shorter and thus had obvious appeal. But she would be on unfamiliar ground. There would be fences, hedges, crops. One of the fields had wheat in it she seemed to recall. The kind of noise she would make in that would surely attract attention very quickly. Or there might be animals to disturb. Cows lurching up out of the darkness, mooing in fear, while she stood in a fear greater than they could understand while Inwit and Plowman homed on the sound.

No. Round the Point it was. She knew that route well. It was longer, but much much safer, she decided. And, having decided, she felt strangely reluctant to move.

It was comfortable crouching here. Familiar almost. The bushes gave her some measure of protection from the rain. She felt well hidden.

It's movement that's dangerous, she heard some part of herself saying. If I stay here nice and quietly, I'll be safe. I won't even need to be here all night. Someone will come looking for me.

Who?

The question rang so loudly in her mind she wondered if she had spoken it out loud. The answer trickled into her mind with a sibilant slowness.

No one will miss me. No one will come looking.

Except Inwit and Plowman.

I've been sitting here long enough, she thought. Too long perhaps.

She pushed herself up from the crouch like a swimmer on the turn, took a single step forward, discovered she had developed cramp as her knee buckled under her.

The movement saved her. There was a sharp explosion and a spurt of flame a few yards away which lit up the beaded lines of driving rain and gave her a brief glimpse of the figure behind. Something plucked at her parka hood. A swarm of small insects seemed to go whistling through the bushes. Then she was off, cramp forgotten, scuttling bent double like a chimpanzee, dreading to hear the second barrel which would send small lines of fire drilling through her back.

It didn't come. Perhaps only one barrel was loaded. Perhaps he was short of ammunition.

Perhaps the further she ran towards the Point, the happier her pursuers were.

The Point. A good place for a murder. A desolate spot where the signs of habitation — Anthorn across the estuaries of the Waver and Wampool. Dumfriesshire across the Solway — merely served to accentuate its own separateness and isolation.

The Point. A headland. A ness. Skinburness. An odd kind of name, meaning . . . she didn't really want to remember its meaning, but it pushed its long length insidiously into her mind. The castle of the headland of the demon. God! She could give the author of that history a chapter full of new horrors.

From the darkness of the ground before her a dozen shapes leapt violently up and shouted mockingly, hoarsely at her.

She stopped with such violence that she fell heavily to the earth and the shriek in her throat was jarred out as a broken rattle. It turned into a whimper of hysterical relief as she recognised her assailants for what they were. Sheep. They had turned instantly and leapt away into the darkness.

But *they* would have heard too. Her every move seemed to be charted as a motorway on a road map. Only speed counted, she must put her trust in speed. She was young, fit, lightly clad. *They* were middle-aged, dressed in heavy clothes, which must be sodden by now, and rubber boots. She could outpace them surely with ease. If she just kept her head. Direction was all important. Visibility was almost down to nil. But she had just to keep the sea on her left. As long as she did that she couldn't go wrong.

She set off at a jog-trot again. She knew where the sea was; she was absolutely certain, but down in the hollows where the paths ran she had been unable to see it, and now she angled her run to the left, suddenly desperate for reassurance that she hadn't somehow turned and headed back towards her pursuers.

The rain lashed into her face, forcing her to close her eyes to the merest slits. She could hear nothing but water, the hiss of the rain as it foamed through the coarse sea-grass and somewhere the deeper, stronger surge and pull of the tide. But the noise seemed all around her and she could not tell whether it grew stronger or weaker.

Then there were sand and stones beneath her feet and she sensed rather than saw the vast openness of the Solway before her.

159

She shielded her eyes from the rain and now she could make out the pale line where the waters were running up the shore, breaking here and there with faint flashes of fluorescence. For a few yards she moved along the beach, but the noise of the stones beneath her feet, the sense of being out in the open plus the sheer discomfort of running on such a surface soon drove her back to the grass-line and the turf.

A flash filled the sky ahead of her. For a second all she could think of was the shot-gun. But the crash that followed almost instantly was the crack of thunder, not the simple bang of a cartridge.

That's all I needed, she thought. They're really laying it on tonight — corpses in the ground, guns, attempted murder, the headland of the demon, and now a real giant-size storm!

As though submitting itself for her approval the lightning ran crazily through the sky overhead like cracks in ancient marble, and the thunder boomed and broke with an almost human gusto.

Emily was pleased to find she could still be entertained. Storms held no fear for her, and in normal circumstances she would have been delighted to stand and watch such a display of natural pyrotechnics. Now she was very conscious of the double-edged aid offered by the lightning. It helped her get her bearings; indeed for seconds at a time the landscape around was lit up clear as daylight, though clarity was the only quality this ghastly, shimmering light shared with the familiar brightness of day. But this meant that she was as visible to anyone else as her surroundings were to her.

She dropped to the ground and peered back during the next flash. Bushes, grass, paths, backed by waving trees and boiling clouds, but no human figure. She set off running again, bent low. When the next flash came, she dropped again to the ground. Ahead she made out in the glare the squat roundness of the pill-box which stood, a memorial to a war which never came near here, right on the Point. She used this as a mark and ran straight at it in the following darkness.

Another flash. The box sat there a hundred yards ahead, squat and sinister. The cairn on top of it seemed grotesque, misshapen. Like an old weather-eaten tombstone.

The lightning seemed to play around the sky for a good half-minute, dying away reluctantly, flickering up again when it seemed gone.

Like old-fashioned footlights, thought Emily, her eyes fixed on the crouching black pill-box. It's a show. Childe Roland to the dark tower came! Tarantara!

It was dark. She set off full pelt, careless of the ground beneath her feet. Her examination had revealed no obstacles. Once round the box, it was a straight run on a good path down along the creek to the safety of the hotel.

The box was further than she thought.

Nearly there! She gasped encouragingly to herself. Nearly nearly nearly there.

She had almost made it when the next flash came and down she dropped. It was less than ten yards away, no longer sinister now she could see the crumbling brickwork and the mossy window slits and the stones in the cairn.

Part of the cairn, the bit that had seemed misshapen and askew, detached itself from the rest and leapt lightly down towards her. For a second this seemed so absurd that she just lay, staring in disbelief.

The demon?

It had an axe. Did demons have axes?

Inwit.

The light went out as he reached her.

She came up fast towards him as the trenching tool swung down and his arms crashed into her left shoulder, forcing her down once more.

He went over the fields and came round by the creek, she thought, feeling somehow like a child who had been cheated. You silly, silly bitch!

She had her arms round him now, keeping close so that he could not swing his weapon at her again. They spun round and round as he tried to throw her clear, but she hung on dizzily as though it were some crazy dance. Neither spoke a word. The only sounds were the thudding and slithering of their feet on the sodden turf and the hiss and strain of desperate breathing. After a few moments Inwit had dropped the tool to free both his hands for the in-fighting. His body had looked weedy enough when she glimpsed him through the hotel door, but it had a wiry strength which was proving more than a match for her. She remembered the casual ease with which he had dealt with her the previous night (she was certain now it had been

Inwit) and knew that once he had freed himself from her clinging grip, she was lost.

Her arms were round his waist, her forehead level with his chin. She tried to straighten her legs to lift him off the ground, but he resisted this move with ease. His hands had been trying to push her clear. Now one of them went snaking round behind her, seized her long blonde hair and pulled. Her head was dragged slowly back from the protective closeness of his chest till her face looked almost vertically up into his. He looked quite unchanged, a little flustered perhaps, but basically as cold and unemotional as ever.

He nodded down at her, as though casually acknowledging her presence, then smashed his forehead down on to her nose.

The pain was terrifying. Tears flooded her eyes till she felt the balls must be washed out and roll down her cheeks. She was sure that her nose was pressed flat against her face. But she still did not let go till his forehead came down again.

Now she went backwards, pushing as hard as possible, reacting instinctively now, all reason sunk fathoms deep in pain. He had been leaning backwards against her weight and the sudden release sent him a couple of steps back and he sat down as a tussock of grass caught at his feet.

Emily didn't sit. She fell, sprawling full length on her back, and looked up at the heavens into a wet darkness. She might have been blind for all she could see. The next flash of lightning convinced her she wasn't. It ran wild pulsating veins of light over the whole dome of the sky. She raised her head.

Inwit was on his feet and coming in for the kill.

She dragged herself up on one knee, her fingers scrabbling in the grass as they had done the night before, desperately searching for a stone, a piece of wood. Anything. Anything.

'Please God!' she sobbed.

She felt the smooth wooden shaft of the trenching tool.

And brought it up with one sweeping movement between Inwit's legs as he stood over her. He emitted a thin high-pitched scream and doubled up like a button-hook before her.

What have I got to do with button-hooks? wondered Emily as she set off once more. She didn't dare touch her nose, which still pained horribly. She marvelled that she could still run and wondered if Inwit's recovery would be as rapid.

She wasn't going to wait to find out. She wasn't going to stop for anything.

The lightning came again, more distant now, but burning bright still.

She stopped dead.

'Stupid, stupid, stupid!' she cried out loud. She had done what she had feared before, lost her sense of direction, and instead of rounding the Point, she had somehow struck off to the left again and was now on the edge of the grassy foreshore overlooking the beach down to the Solway.

This was quite near the spot where she had

lain out in the sun and woken to find the marks of Scott's horse around her. For a second her mind was diverted from her own predicament to consider how and where Michael Scott might be.

Some magician! she sneered, then disliked herself intensely as the image of the blood starting out of his shoulder and his face, suddenly white, high above the pain-maddened rearing horse, came into her mind.

She sneezed and the pain of sneezing brought her back to herself.

Perhaps her mistake might prove to her advantage. If she kept low and doubled back along the edge of the beach she could surely outwit them. Inwit was out of the hunt, temporarily at least. And Plowman would surely expect her to be making for the path along the creek. It was all so simple. Suddenly, absurdly she felt almost safe.

'It was most considerate of you to sneeze, Mrs. Follett,' said a pleasantly hearty voice behind her. 'I might have missed you else.'

It was Plowman, of course, standing a couple of yards away, the shot-gun levelled steadily at her midriff.

She turned and ran towards the sea. The tide was coming in fast and the water was only about twenty-five yards away.

She expected to hear the shot almost instantly. She had seen at the cinema the damage a shot-gun could do. She had no reason to believe it was exaggerated

When it didn't come, she wondered for an optimistic second if her earlier surmise had been right and Plowman was short of ammunition. But a glance over her shoulder showed him walking steadily behind her and she knew then exactly what he was doing.

He was saving himself a job. Not for her the dubious dignity of burial in the gorse bushes. He was going to shoot her in the shallows, then leave the incoming tide to suck her out to sea.

She acted on the thought, turned right and accelerated with all her remaining strength, running parallel to the water.

Behind her, Plowman turned too, half stumbling in the loose stones which littered the sand. Then the gun came up to his shoulder. It was time to finish it.

Emily changed direction again, left this time, straight down into the water. She brought her knees up high to lessen resistance, ran as far as she could into a depth of about a yard, and flung herself forward.

Behind her the gun cracked, slightly double, and the air above her hissed momentarily.

Both barrels. He had meant to make a job of it. How long to reload? She swung her arms over desperately, forgetting the long easy stroke which had made her her school's distance champion from the age of thirteen on. Distance she would want shortly. At present speed was everything.

A dozen strokes she promised herself. Just a dozen.

. . . Eight, nine, ten, eleven, twelve. One for luck. Then down in a steep dive. The bottom not far. Still no real depth. Swim steadily down here. Change of direction so he couldn't follow the line. Lungs beginning to strain now. A little longer. Not too long though. Don't want to explode to the surface. Just up gently. Hardly break it. One deep breath and . . .

A foot in front of her face the water boiled momentarily as hot shot screwed viciously into it. He was nearer than she would have believed possible, almost up to his waist. He must have guessed she would turn and swim along with the tide.

This time she stayed down till her lungs almost burst, came up like a dolphin, straight back under, kicking hard all the time away from the shore. Twice more and she risked a glance back. In the rain and the darkness the shore was quite invisible.

Now she settled down into the long easy stroke which came naturally to her, conserving her energy from time to time by treading water and letting the considerable momentum of the tide sweep her along. After twenty minutes, perhaps more, she could no longer tell, the storm had moved away and the rain died down to a steady drizzle. Suddenly she thought she made out a dark shape on the water and heard the creaking of rowlocks. She dived instantly, remembering the boats which lay along the edge of the creek and fearing that Inwit and Plowman might have stolen one to continue the search.

Surfacing again, she decided she must have been mistaken as a large wave lifted her up and gave her a reasonably clear view of the sea ahead. She slid down into the trough and turned on her back, trying to conserve her energy and at the same time give herself some sense of direction if the wind had torn a gap in the clouds for the stars to shine through.

It hadn't. Another wave rose above her threatening to break over her body. She was unworried knowing she would be driven before it or lifted upon it. Unworried till cutting its crest she saw the broad prow of a rowing boat.

It was purely fortuitous, she told herself as she duck-dived. They weren't trying to run me down, they couldn't even know I was there. They were bloody lucky to get within a mile of me. Perhaps it wasn't even them.

She came up for air, heard the now almost familiar bang, saw the water immediately ahead pocked with more violence than the rain could cause, and went under once more.

It was them all right. Plowman again, Inwit could hardly be thinking coherently yet, clever fat little Plowman knowing she'd move with the tide; so he played the odds and had been sitting out in the estuary waiting for her to show up.

This time she came up almost alongside the boat. A wave tipped it towards her and she saw the inmates quite clearly. Inwit was straining at the oars, using them for balance rather than propulsion, while his partner peered menacingly over the prow, shot-gun at the ready.

Inwit saw her first and screamed something. What he said was inaudible in the wind and rain, but the noise attracted Plowman, who turned, saw Emily, and moved rapidly towards her. She watched his awkward bobbing approach for a second, then seized the side of the boat and

168

forced herself up out of the water. The sudden intensification of the already considerable rocking action took Plowman by surprise. He stumbled to his knees, slid towards the side of the boat and let go of the gun as he grabbed the gunwale to stop himself from going over.

Emily reached casually down, picked up the gun and flung herself backwards into the sea. Treading water, she brandished the still gleaming weapon over her head with sudden memories of Excalibur flooding her triumphant mind, and let it slide slowly down into the waves. Plowman shouting inaudible abuse wrenched one of the oars from Inwit and lifted it up in a final effort to deliver a death blow. Inwit's mouth funnelled in a panic-stricken warning; the boat, relieved of one of its restraining arms, bounded high aslant the next wave; the other oar, traitor now it was alone, exaggerated the perilous steepness of the angle by burying itself too deep for Inwit to hold it, and effortlessly the swelling waters flipped the boat over.

Only one head broke the surface, too far away for Emily to see whose it was. She swam with all possible speed towards it, but while she was still yards short, another wave crashed down and sank it from view.

She moved in a circle for a while, watching to see if anyone appeared again. She could see the capsized boat quite close, but there was no one clinging to it. She dived underneath to make sure neither of the men was trapped, and after that, knowing it was almost certainly hopeless,

169

she dived deep and searched till her lungs could bear no more.

When she came to the surface again even the boat had gone. There was nothing but herself and the water, sweeping her she knew not where. She had used a great deal of vital energy, and was beginning to feel very cold. She had discarded her parka and her shoes as soon as possible, and her sweater and slacks were beginning to weigh more and more heavily. It was time to make a landfall.

This proved more difficult than she would have imagined. Eventually visibility improved sufficiently for her to get a bearing on the tall red-lighted masts at the Anthorn naval base. But this was only a vague help, as there was nothing to indicate from which angle she was seeing them. Occasionally as she trod water she felt the bottom underfoot, but this always proved to be merely sandbanks, and sometimes the sand was suspiciously ready to yield to her weight. She decided to keep afloat as long as possible till she was sure of her footing.

When she finally came ashore she knew at once where she was, and didn't like it. She was somewhere on Skinburness salt marsh, several acres of desolate turf-land cut through with tidal ditches and creeks which could swallow a man effortlessly. She had come here once on an unsuccessful early-morning mushrooming trip. In the grey light of morning the place had seemed uninviting enough. Now, almost invisible, it seemed doubly so.

She shivered violently and felt her muscles

beginning to stiffen. Uninviting or not, the marsh had to be crossed. From what she recalled, the surface was firm enough, pleasant, springy Solway turf much of it, greatly in demand for lawns and football pitches. What needed care were the steep-sided creeks and inlets. Even the greatest swimming ability was little use when you had ten feet of sheer, slippery mud to traverse to get back to the surface. And at the moment she felt her own swimming potential much diminished. She was going to move very carefully.

Five minutes later she was splashing in a dead panic at the bottom of a very narrow, very steep ditch. Her eyes were no longer to be trusted, it seemed. The ground ahead had seemed as firm and trustworthy as that on which she stood. Only there hadn't been any ground there, just a hole.

The water was only about five feet deep, but it was impossible to stand in it. The bottom seemed to consist of voracious oily mud which sucked at her feet and seemed to her overwrought imagination ready and able to pull her completely under. But getting out proved as difficult as she had foreseen. Twice she nearly made it when the rim of the ditch crumbled away under her weight and she slithered back down. The third time she utilised the ditch's narrowness which before had seemed a positive hindrance, and forced herself up like a climber in a chimney, her feet pressing against one side, her back against the other.

She almost succeeded. She seemed to be lying

across the ditch at ground level when the wall behind her back just seemed to cave in and her head and shoulders began a downward slither.

Worse, her feet had somehow been thrust so deep into the mud of the other side that she could not free them and for a ghastly second she feared she was going to be suspended upside down in the murky waters below.

'Help! Help me!' she cried for the first time since this evening had all begun. Even as she shouted the thought crossed her mind that she was less likely to be heard here than almost anywhere else she had been that night, not even excepting the Solway.

Then her arms were caught from above and she was lifted bodily out of the ditch. She turned, still fearing Inwit or Plowman, turned and looked and almost wished it was one of those two.

She was being held up by a green man, her knees buckled beneath her, his face became hazy. But her mind absurdly, ridiculously, refused to lose its hold on consciousness despite all the encouragement it received, not even when he lifted her up into his arms and began to move swiftly, efficiently over the marsh.

To his lair, she thought. We're going to his lair. He wants to share me with the rest of the family.

There was something macabrely amusing in the thought, like a vulture making a good mother.

He stopped and began to lower her into a hole in the ground.

She looked down.

In the hole looking up, and reaching up to receive her, were half a dozen more green men.

At last she could faint.

8

The next few hours reminded her strongly of her attempts to evade Plowman in the sea. Long periods in the still, dark world beneath the water interspersed by brief moments above the surface where anything, or nothing, could happen.

She broke the surface lightly for a second to realise she was still out in the open air and the men were undressing her. Quickly she submerged again. Next in a strange room by a bed. She was dressed now, or rather wrapped, in a strange green-coloured garment; she was being undressed again, by a woman this time.

Better, she thought. Or perhaps worse? as she slipped under again.

Someone fiddling with her nose dragged her protesting upwards once more. The woman was still there. It was Nurse Simpson, she decided without interest or surprise.

Down again.

It was nice down there this time. There was a beautifully sensuous dream in which she lay in bed with six green men. She wasn't afraid of them any more. They were marvellous. She felt she had to tell them and touched one on the shoulder. He winced with pain. Her hand was tacky with blood. She looked at his face. Sad, despairing, almost lifeless, it was Michael Scott.

She broke the surface with a great splash this time, left the depths clear behind, and sat up in bed determined to plunge no more.

Nurse Simpson came through the door as though on command.

'I want to get up,' said Emily, trying to be firm, but sounding to her own ears only like a petulant child in a sickbed.

'Put this on,' said Simpson without showing any emotion. She might have been Inwit's sister.

Perhaps she is, thought Emily.

The woman took a dress from a wall cupboard. It was grey, high-necked, with a white bow at the breast. Quite hideous.

Emily stepped out of bed and found she was wearing a cotton night-dress. She had half expected to find herself weak and dizzy, but except for a certain amount of stiffness she felt surprisingly strong.

'Your underclothes are dry,' said Simpson. 'They are hanging over the chair. There's a bathroom through that door.'

On that, she turned and left the room.

Emily dressed as fast as she could. The only footgear she could find was a pair of slippers a size too large for her. The dress proved to be as hideous as she had first thought, tight around the bust, floppy round the waist, and hideously long. She went through into the bathroom in search of a mirror. Her hair felt a mess.

But when she looked into the small mirror fixed on to the door of the bathroom cabinet it wasn't her hair that held her attention, it was her nose.

A wedge of pink lint was folded over it, held in place by three strips of plaster running from cheek to cheek. She could not understand how she had not noticed this before. Once observed in the mirror, the whole assembly began to itch and tickle abominably. With the itch there also came a surge of the curiosity tinged with fear which had been oddly lacking since she awoke.

I suppose, she thought, after last night, anything vaguely resembling normality is going to seem too attractive to be questioned.

But now she went to the window and tried to look out. It was frosted glass and when she tried to open it she found the catch was stuck.

She set off back into the bedroom to open the curtains, but stopped short in the bathroom doorway.

Standing at the foot of the bed was a young man.

He smiled approvingly at her. She was sure she had not met him before, yet he looked strangely familiar.

'Good morning, Mrs. Follett,' he said. 'I hope I'm not intruding.'

'As I don't know the house rules here, I can't say,' answered Emily.

'You seem to have made a good recovery,' he said happily. 'I have come to take you down to breakfast if you are ready.'

'Well, I'm certainly hungry, if that's what you mean.'

She moved casually over to the curtained window, but he stepped in front of her and offered his arm.

'Shall we go, then?'

She shrugged. 'Why not?'

176

Outside the door she found herself in a long, rather dark corridor which ran between pairs of anonymous doors at about four-yard intervals. She thought that one or two of these were opened just fractionally, enough to permit anyone inside to peer out. She thought of stumbling against one to test her theory when the corridor broadened out into quite a roomy landing and they turned left down a flight of stairs. After turning at a couple of half-landings she found herself descending into a mosaically tiled hallway utterly devoid of ornament or furniture. Only the fine oak doors which opened off it prevented it from looking too like a public lavatory.

And even those just needed a penny-in-the-slot lock to fit the picture, thought Emily with a giggle which must have been almost audible as her young escort gave her a curious glance.

The click of his leather-soled shoes on the tiled floor reminded her of her own footwear.

'I hope we're not expecting too many guests at breakfast,' she murmured.

Again that curious glance. He did not reply, however, but went over to one of the doors, knocked gently, opened it (whether or not at an invitation from inside, Emily was not sure) and looked in.

'Mrs. Follett, sir,' he said.

Then he stood aside, motioned Emily to go in, and closed the door behind her.

It was a beautiful room, high-ceilinged, papered in exquisite taste, with a large richly curtained window looking out on a small lawn and rose garden, while in the wall opposite was set a finely proportioned Adam, or pseudo-Adam, fireplace, beside which stood a man.

In the centre of the room was a large table set for breakfast. On the sideboard against the wall to the left of the window was a variety of silver tureens from which another man was filling a plate. There were two others seated at the table, already eating.

But Emily had little eye for the beauties of the room or the breakfasting men. Her gaze was fixed steadily on the man by the fireplace and his was returned just as steadily.

It was the man she had run away from (the old-fashioned phrase came easily to her mind) some three weeks earlier. Her husband, Sterne Follett.

'Ah. Emily,' he said, as though she had just come into a drawing room where he was coping alone with early guests. Just a touch of reproof, audible only to the tuned-in ear.

He moved and came across to her and kissed her lightly on the cheek near the ends of the plaster strips. He was unchanged. Not that there was any reason why he should have changed. It was less than a month since she had left him. But it seemed years ago, and she felt herself so completely altered that it seemed anachronistic to see him standing before her, smiling courteously as ever; his thick brown hair exquisitely groomed, with just sufficient grey over the temple to display modestly the defeat of age; his intelligent, handsome face showing all the lines of maturity, but none of the flabbiness;

178

his clear brown eyes scrutinising her point by point; his clothing as ever immaculate in cut, muted in colour, with just a hint of flamboyance in the small yellow rose he affected in his buttonhole. All this was so familiar to Emily in her past and so strange and out of place in the future she had planned for herself that her head began spinning, and she felt herself as dizzy and unready as the naive eighteen-year-old girl who a decade earlier had stood dazzled in front of the same man for the first time.

He took her unresisting arm and led her gently towards the others.

'My dear,' he said. 'Let me present my friends to you. Gentlemen, I would like you to meet my wife.'

The 'gentleman' by the sideboard was ungentlemanly enough to raise his eyebrows in surprise, though whether at her presence or her appearance Emily wasn't sure. The other two stood up and Sterne led her slowly round the table, for all the world, thought Emily, beginning to recover slightly, like the Queen at a Royal Command Performance.

'Colonel Petard,' said Sterne, pausing before the first.

'How do you do, Colonel,' said Emily, finding herself, despite everything, beginning to enter into the ridiculous charade. This always happened with Sterne. This was his great strength. Negotiations were conducted under his terms, games played to his rules. It was easier that way. In the past it had usually seemed impossible any other way. Colonel Petard, a small, rather exaggeratedly military man with a horrid moustache and a poker-straight bearing, obviously played to the rules, as did the next, Major Glover, younger, handsomer, more relaxed. He might have been at a hunt ball. They both took her hand, inclined their heads over it, and murmured the ritual exchanges of meeting and greeting.

The third man, standing by the sideboard, was obviously built on other lines. Long, rangy, thin-faced, with a sharp nose and narrow shrewd eyes, he was introduced as Mr. Conn. He made no attempt to take her hand, but continued to help himself to bacon.

'Hello, Mrs. Follett,' he said with a sharp New York accent. His eyes ran openly from her plastered nose via the hideous dress down to her overlarge fluffy slippers.

He's not going to play, thought Emily, and the thought delighted her. She tightened her lips against a grin, but his quick glance caught it and a slow smile began to spread over his face.

'You must give me the name of your dressmaker,' he said, and started to laugh.

She found herself laughing with him, almost doubled up with merriment. At the same time she carefully listened for any telltale note of hysteria, but was delighted to detect only a stream of pure, unadulterated mirth.

As it died away, Sterne spoke, mildly, politely. 'Will you join us for breakfast, my dear?'

Back to the game.

'Yes, please,' she said gaily. 'I'm starving.'

She seized a plate, piled it up quickly,

efficiently, and took a seat at the table. She began to eat with gusto, pausing only to say to her husband, 'Pour me a cup of coffee, there's a love.'

The others continued their breakfasts in a polite silence. Once she caught Mr. Conn's eye and half choked on a kidney. She felt gay, almost drunk, ready to carry the attack to her husband.

Her plate empty, she tore a slice of bread in half, carefully wiped the remnants of egg, fat, and sauce from her plate with it, ate it and gently licked her fingers.

'I'm glad we bumped into each other like this, love,' she said, pushing the plate from her with a satisfied sigh, feeling absolutely ready for attack. 'I began to get worried when I didn't hear from your solicitor.'

He looked quite unperturbed, gave a slight nod, but didn't speak, so she had to go on without a cue. He might at least have said 'my solicitor' in a surprised voice.

'About the divorce,' she said. 'I thought I would have heard something by now.'

'You're getting a divorce?' said Conn with a perceptible note of disbelief, looking at Sterne.

He knows my boy, thought Emily. Let's see which way you jump now.

'My dear,' said Sterne quietly, the note of reproof back just a little nearer the surface now, 'I'm surprised you wish to discuss personal matters in the circumstances. I thought you might have been more concerned with the fate of Mr. Scott.'

181

Suddenly the sense of gaiety and strength left Emily. Sterne had turned everything upside down once more. She wanted to scream violent abuse at him, but at herself also. The reproof was well administered.

'What about him?' she asked anxiously. 'I had almost forgotten. I'm sorry. How is he?'

Sterne shrugged.

'We hoped you might tell us, my dear. Last night you talked incoherently a great deal before the sedative administered to you took effect. Among other things, you said Scott had been wounded. Men have been out searching all night. His horse has been found, its neck badly grazed with shot, wandering by the edge of the sea. Of its rider there is no sign.'

'Oh God!' said Emily.

'How badly hurt was he, Mrs. Follett?' asked Petard abruptly.

'I don't know. In the shoulder, here.' She touched her left shoulder and looked at her hand, remembering her dream.

'He may have fallen off in the shallows,' said Major Glover musingly. 'Then as the tide came in, he'd just, well, disappear.'

Emily swayed slightly in her seat. Conn shot Glover an angry glance.

'Look,' he said, 'I'm the outsider here, O.K. But I reckon we should first of all get Mrs. Follett to tell us exactly what happened last night instead of just relying on what she said when she was brought in.'

'If you wish,' said Sterne, as if it was a matter of no interest at all to him. He moved back to his former position by the fireplace.

Rapidly, economically, Emily described what had happened the night before, starting at her expedition in search of the grave of Fenimore Castell.

'Then,' she concluded, 'I was picked up by a . . . by a green man. God, I'd almost forgotten about him, them, and brought here, I presume. Why, though? Who or what are they? And what is this place, anyway?'

'Later, later,' said Conn impatiently. 'Listen, Emily, what happened before all this? There must be more. Why did you come to Skinburness in the first place?'

Emily looked steadily at Sterne, who once again steadily returned her gaze. What did he want her to say? she wondered.

'Escape,' she said. 'I had left Sterne. I wanted to hide somewhere for a while.'

Strange, it did not seem incongruous or embarrassing to be sitting here in front of strangers talking about her private life, her desires, fears, hopes.

'No,' said Conn, patiently. 'I didn't mean that.'

'What we want to know,' barked Petard suddenly, as if he had decided it was time for a display of military efficiency, 'is why Skinburness? Didn't you know of your husband's connection with the college?'

'No,' said Emily firmly, glad to be able to speak the absolute truth.

Petard and Glover exchanged a glance of disbelief.

'Had I known,' added Emily, 'it would have

been the last place on earth I would have chosen.'

This wasn't absolute truth, perhaps, but enough to be going on with.

Conn nodded as if this made sense, the other two looked hard at her as if they would have liked to open up her mind and peer in.

'You do admit you knew your husband knew *of* Skinburness as a place?' Glover asked politely.

'Yes. Of course. I mentioned it to him as a place I'd like to revisit. I used to come here as a child. He seemed a little surprised when I mentioned the name. Almost startled. Then amused. He said he didn't think it was such a good idea to revisit the scenes of youthful pleasure. He said Skinburness meant the headland near the castle of the demon. Some demons didn't hurt children, but let them fatten into adults before they took them. It was better to let sleeping demons die.'

She glanced across at Sterne as though for confirmation, but he didn't move or speak. A thin thread of smoke drifted up from the cigarette he had lit now they had finished eating. He was meticulous in his concern for the comfort of others — in little things. She wondered how he felt standing in the background listening to an interrogation which so closely concerned himself. She suspected he *felt* nothing, his reaction was purely cerebral. And it was beginning to dawn on her that she was here in this room at the instigation of the others, not of Sterne.

Conn nodded once more.

184

'It's a lonely place,' he said.

'Look,' said Emily. 'What's all this about? I am, I take it, in the college?'

They nodded somberly. The Colonel looked at Major Glover who began speaking.

'We'll stick to you for the moment, if you don't mind, Mrs. Follett. You can see our problem. Either you're in Skinburness purely by accident or you are here by design.'

'Applause, applause,' said Emily.

Glover went on unperturbed.

'This could either be your own design, because you know of Mr. Follett's connection with the place and wish to make capital out of your knowledge. Alternatively, it could, of course, be by Mr. Follett's own design.'

There it was now. Spelt out clearly. Sterne was on the hook, not wriggling and struggling, but hanging there passively till the moment came to break completely loose. Why and how didn't matter. What did she owe him? That was the question. And just how important was her silence? She had to know a lot more before she could decide. Time was the thing.

'I don't know if it will help or hinder my husband,' she said steadily, 'but it was my own free decision to come here. If we had arranged it together why would it have been necessary to arrange for me to be spied on?'

'Spied on?' said Conn, surprised.

'You mean the man Burgess,' said the Colonel, almost apologetically. He looked at Sterne, who raised his eyebrows quizzically.

'I'm sorry, sir,' said the Colonel. 'The

185

switchboard sergeant was naturally curious about the calls. He did a bit of checking back. I disciplined him, of course, but intelligence, however obtained, is intelligence.'

Sterne nodded understandingly, a quiet smile on his lips.

'Purely a marital matter, you understand, Petard. Things have not been well. I'm sorry, my dear.'

This did not match up to the Follett image at all, thought Emily. An explanation, followed by an apology! The implied lie was to be expected, however.

She glanced at the others to see if they had noticed.

'This man Burgess,' said Conn. 'What is he? Some kind of private eye?'

A pained look crossed Sterne's face.

'Arthur Burgess is an old and trusted employee of mine, an executive of some considerable status.'

'Nothing to do with the set-up here, eh?' barked Petard.

'As you so obviously know, Colonel. Nothing to do with the college side of my business.'

'You sure make your executives earn their dough,' said Conn, an edge of scorn in his voice.

'Mr. Conn, please,' said the Colonel. 'You are a guest.'

'Oh God! The English!' said Conn, throwing his arms out in mock despair.

'Perhaps I might remind you,' said Glover urbanely. 'If there had been a little more English

186

common sense, and a little less super-duper-American-swingalong security among your people, we wouldn't be here now.'

'Stop squabbling, please,' said Sterne sharply. He moved forward from the fireplace and held everyone in his gaze.

He's going to take over again, thought Emily. He's picked his moment. I don't understand what the hell's going on, but Sterne's gathering up the strings again.

'I think,' said her husband, 'that I have stood aside from my responsibilities for long enough, Colonel. It is always unfortunate in our business when the domestic overlaps with the professional. I realise it is necessary you satisfy yourself this is accidental. On the other hand, much remains to be done.'

'Of course, sir. You appreciate it was necessary. I did not wish to work behind your back.'

'I appreciate that, Colonel Petard.'

'Christ!' said Conn. 'O.K., so we're happy that Mrs. Follett is here by a dirty great coincidence. So perhaps we can stop scratching each other's backs and get down to business.'

'Thank you, Mr. Conn. Would you mind opening the door and asking Captain Carruthers to step inside?'

That's you reduced to serf status, Mr. Conn! thought Emily sympathetically.

Conn caught her eye, grinned, and went to the door. The young man who had brought Emily downstairs came in at his call.

'Captain,' said Sterne, 'please take Mrs. Follett back to her room. See she is comfortable and has everything she wants.'

'Oh no,' said Emily. 'I'm comfortable right here. And what I want is simple. I want to know what the hell's going on. I'm entitled to know. I've got bruises to prove it. You can make it short or you can make it long. But here I stay till I'm in the picture, as you might put it, Colonel.'

There was a heavy silence.

'She's right,' said Conn suddenly. 'Hell, it's not my business, but you've got to tell her something.'

He glared around defiantly, but there was no resistance.

'Of course,' said Sterne. 'But we need not detain you here, my dear. Who better than Captain Carruthers to tell the story? Captain, you heard? Take my wife upstairs and put her in the picture; that was, I think, the phrase? Try not to contravene too much of the Official Secrets Act, there's a good fellow. In fact, perhaps you should get her to sign first.'

Carruthers came smartly to attention and opened the door with a polite bow to Emily. Reluctantly she rose.

'All right,' she said. 'But if I am not satisfied I'll be back. Good morning, gentlemen.'

Back in her room she was amused but not surprised when Carruthers brought her a paper to sign. Sterne did not make jokes. It was a digest of the Official Secrets Act. She glanced quickly over it, then signed a printed statement saying that she had read and understood. Something of her earlier frivolity remained and she had to restrain herself from adding a line of kisses under her name.

Kisses somehow made her think again of Michael Scott, and as before the thought sobered her. For some reason comparisons of Scott and Sterne started rising in her mind. Sterne's courtesy, Scott's rudeness; Sterne's elegance, Scott's casualness; Sterne pecking at her cheek, Scott's face white with pain above the rearing horse. Sterne alive, outliving everything, everyone, a natural survivor; and Scott washed bloatedly ashore by Blitterlees or Wolsty Bank.

Carruthers was looking at her patiently, ready to start when she was. She forced herself back to the present.

'Right, Captain,' she said. 'Simple things first. Just what is this place?'

'The college?' he said with a smile. 'Why, it's what the name implies. A college. A place where people are trained.'

'Trained for what?'

'Really, I suppose, it's a kind of military training. Men come here who have been selected as suitable for a rather specialised kind of job.'

He sat down opposite, balanced precariously on a rickety-looking chair, and seemed ready to warm to his task.

'What do you know about your husband, Mrs. Follett? About his job, I mean?'

'His job?' Emily was surprised. 'Well, I know that he's an enormously wealthy man, that he has a controlling financial interest in several companies. He has a suite of offices in Davies Street off Oxford Street, where he spends much of his time in London. But he seems to spend

189

more travelling around Europe on some kind of business trips — making top-level contacts is the nearest I've heard him get to describing his work. All I knew was that it usually involved dining with a lot of very important, very boring people.'

Her mind went back to those trips. France, Italy, Austria, behind the Curtain. She was being unfair, stressing the boring people. Not all had been boring. And she had seen the world in a style and at a level she had never dreamed possible even in her most extravagant adolescent fantasies. Too much style, perhaps. Too high a level.

'Sterne seemed to collect influence like other people collect match-boxes or stamps.'

She realised she had spoken aloud. Some vestigial sense of loyalty made her sorry, sorry at least that she had spoken thus in front of a subordinate about his boss.

'Sterne is your boss, isn't he?' she suddenly asked.

'Why yes. He is. He is the one behind it all. He is the one responsible,' said Carruthers. 'Listen. Mr. Follett's trips abroad were all they seemed to be. But a little more also. You see, your husband is more than just a collector of influence, he's a man of action too. He is also employed by one of our security services.'

He paused, as though waiting for a dramatic reaction. He wasn't disappointed.

'You mean, Sterne's a spy!' said Emily incredulously.

'No, no,' laughed Carruthers. 'Not in any

sense you mean. No guns, micro-film, beautiful blondes in the boudoir, present company excepted, of course, nothing like that. He is a man of quite exceptional organising talents, as I'm sure you know. That's what made him what he is. His job in security was as a kind of peripatetic organiser. All the strings are gathered in at Whitehall, of course. And on the spot we have our local centres — third secretaries, trade missions, that kind of thing. But from time to time it's invaluable to have a top man on the spot also. Someone who can check up on the local organisation while seeing the overall big picture at the same time.'

'And this has been Sterne's job?'

'Yes. For many years now. And a tremendous success he has made of it. But a few years ago, two or three, it began to be felt that the time had come for a change. One thing's certain in this game. If you go on long enough you'll be found out. Oh, I know you only hear about the ones that get caught, never the ones that are successful. But it's a good basic tenet of belief! Anyway, it wasn't worth the risk exposing your husband to the dangers of trips behind the Curtain any more, not with his vast knowledge of the whole European set-up. So a fade-out job began. Gradually, of course. It's still going on. It's like stalking — one unexpected or violent movement and everything goes running. But you might have noticed you weren't travelling so far so often in recent years?'

Emily nodded slowly. Their journeys to Eastern Europe had become much fewer and more infrequent. Not that she had minded. Despite all her tenaciously retained left-wing views, she was always glad to see those particular frontiers fall behind her.

'Of course, Western Europe still remained. Everybody listens to everybody else. But other work was found for Mr. Follett also. He is too valuable a man to be kept even in partial indolence. One of his new babies was this place.'

He waved his hand vaguely around.

' 'By indirections find directions out,' ' quoted Emily. 'You mean you're finally going to tell me what this is all about?'

'Certainly. But the preamble was essential as your surprise demonstrated. Well now. The college was until about three years ago a teachers' training college; before that it had been a private residence, I believe. It was too small to be viable as a teachers' college, the Department of Education decided, and they were in the act of closing it down when it came to our notice. I said before that the exotic spy image didn't fit your husband. It doesn't really fit anyone. It's all foreign businessmen as collectors and disaffected natives as retailers. But another kind of operation is often needed. A quick in-and-out. Scrumping, we call it. Over the wall, fill your pockets with apples, then run like hell.'

'Like Commando raids in the war?' asked Emily.

'Yes. Very like. But even more flexible, more expert. More anonymous too. Strictly non-military. That would be an act of war.'

'I don't quite see what purpose . . . '

'Look,' interrupted Carruthers. 'Something odd starts being constructed just over the border from West Germany. You want to know what it is quick. No time to get to a man on the actual job, even if that were possible. So you send a little boarding party to have a look, preferably without being noticed. That needs experts. Real experts. They've got to be good enough to run up the beach at Havana, walk twice around the town and leave before dawn without Fidel's sleep being disturbed.'

'And are they?'

'Just about,' he said, his forehead crinkling into a slight frown. 'That's part of the trouble. Anyway, as you've probably grasped by now, we took over this place as a training centre. It was perfect. Remote without being inaccessible and with enough people around to make constant vigilance an absolute essential. Anyone can wander around in the Scottish Highlands, for instance, thinking they're softer-footed than the last of the Mohicans. Here you're really put to the test. And over on the other side we have a sister establishment.'

He went to the window and pulled open the curtains. Emily blinked into the daylight for a moment. The room was at the front of the college and she was looking out over the Solway to the Scottish shore. The sky was a beautiful shade of eggshell blue. The only sign of the previous night's storm were sparkling droplets of rain which gleamed everywhere in the grass and the bushes below.

'It's a useful arrangement,' said Carruthers. 'It

gives both of us a target on training raids. And as we all know the methods we use, both places devise defence systems to combat these. Which means in turn we devise new methods of circumventing the defences. It's like the public-school house system. A bit of hearty competition sharpens up everyone. There the resemblance ends, I'm glad to say.'

'And Sterne's in charge? But what on earth does he know . . . ?' Her voice tailed away, incredulous at the thought of Sterne running around in the dark with his face blackened and a gun in his hand.

'About this kind of exercise?' Carruthers completed her question. 'In practice, nothing of course. In theory, from what I have heard him say, he has obviously read and taken in everything that's ever been written on the subject. He has a tremendous mind. But his real job has been an organisational one. Getting the idea off the ground, finance, establishment, selection of personnel, siting. It's been a tremendous job, especially when it's been done more or less part time. And he has made a real go of it. There are two others as well. One in the Lake District, one in Northern Ireland. We cover a wide variety of terrains.'

'What's gone wrong, then?' Emily asked, anxious to get to the meat of the matter.

And what's happened to Michael? And what's being done about Inwit and Plowman? And has anyone gone to dig up poor Fenimore Castell?

But she didn't voice these questions, just let them worry their way round and round her mind as she listened to Carruthers.

'Six days ago,' he said, 'a raiding party set out from the college. As always, the man in charge of the party had received sealed orders which he did not open until he reached a pre-ordained spot. In this case it was two miles off shore in one of our rubber dinghies. It seemed certain the objective would be the familiar one of our sister college. Instead when the leader opened his instructions they told him to effect entry to the U.S. naval research base at Caerlaverock. You've probably noticed the lights at night. Look, you can see it now.'

He pointed out across the water. Emily nodded without really looking.

'Go on,' she said.

'Well, orders are orders. The man in charge was puzzled but . . . '

'Stop being coy,' said Emily in exasperation. 'It was you, wasn't it?'

'Why, yes. It was,' said Carruthers with a slow smile. 'How very perceptive.'

'This is why Sterne said you were the obvious man to tell the story.'

'Good thinking! All right. *I* was puzzled, but it seemed not unreasonable. I assumed the go-ahead had been given by the Americans. And indeed we had in the past studied both in the field and on paper the outer defence system of the base. So as an exercise in extemporisation, which we frequently had, it was not all that exceptional.'

'But enough to puzzle you.'

'Yes. Still, on we pressed. There were six of

195

us. About a mile off shore we anchored the dinghy. That is, someone went down to the bottom with a line and hitched it to a rock. Then we all went over the side and headed for the shore.'

A look of revelation swept up into Emily's face.

'You mean, like frogmen? You'd be wearing some kind of . . . ? Well, what colour . . . ?'

Carruthers looked puzzled for a second, then laughed.

'Green! Of course! You and your green men. I thought you'd realised! It's an excellent camouflage colour round here. We have skin-tight suits, a sort of blacky green, and dark green nylon hoods which take away the shape of the face as well as mask the colour.'

'It was you last night who picked me up!'

'Of course. Didn't you know? I've been waiting for maidenly gratitude to rear its head ever since.'

'Later please, Captain.' She smiled at him, liking this young man very much.

'Let's have the end of the story first.'

'Well, to cut it short, we got in with remarkable ease, which was not surprising as we discovered later, got clean through to their central admin block as instructed in our orders, then made our way out again. They would never have known we'd been there, but someone touched off an alarm as we made our way back over the perimeter wire. It's an old lesson, one you can't learn often enough. You've got to be even more careful getting out than in. But it was lucky in a way that night. We went off like the clappers, of course. Their men seemed to spring out of the ground all around us. This didn't worry me till someone put a shot over our heads. Then I worried! But we made it back to the dinghy O.K., got back across to our side in good spirits — you know how you feel invigorated after danger — beached and stowed the dinghy, came back here and were arrested at the front door!'

He paused for effect.

'Go on!' said Emily obligingly.

'Someone, it seemed, while we were in the base, had opened their top-security safe, extracted a small capsule which contained a piece of micro-tape on which was printed information of greater importance than anyone has seen fit to confide to me, and taken this as a souvenir. We were stripped, searched thoroughly, inside and out, which was rather disgusting, and cross-questioned for the rest of the night.'

'But why? I mean, did it have to be one of you? And surely if the Americans agreed to the raid they'd have taken more precautions than they seemed to?'

'Very true,' said Carruthers. 'That was the trouble, you see. They hadn't agreed. And the orders Colonel Petard had sealed up for me didn't mention the base. The ones I opened didn't originate from him. And naturally there wasn't a rush of volunteers to say where they had come from. Anyway, one of us had taken the tape. It seemed a good theory. When we were spotted on the way out the Commandant there put two and two together very quickly. He's quite chummy with the Colonel. So he got on the phone, hence the reception party when we got home. The search produced nothing, so they started on the shore between where we had landed and the college. The trouble was, of course, that we made our way back individually. A little knot of six green men is a bit too obvious! No one had taken an excessive amount of time, but it meant there was a lot of possible ground to cover.'

'Did they find anything?'

'Yes. The capsule. But no sign of the tape. We were all put under arrest. Close, but not too close. They left us room to manoeuvre. You see, the tape hadn't been passed on yet. At least it seemed unlikely. And out of its capsule, exposed to the elements as it probably was, its magnetic field would begin to break down, and within a couple of weeks at the most it would be unusable. So everyone was watching like mad. Mr. Conn arrived the next morning and has been around ever since. The Colonel has been part apologetic, part jubilant at the ease with which we got into the place. But I gather Conn reckons someone over there was in on it and made things easy. It's nice to know they have their traitors too.'

The word hung heavily on the air.

'But tell me,' said Emily. 'You said you were watched all the time, under arrest. Well, why are you wandering around so freely now? And why's Conn still here? And why . . . ?'

All the whys would have come tumbling out of

her then if Carruthers hadn't held up a restraining hand.

'Hold on!' he said. 'Let me finish. The loose rein was too loose. Two nights later one of the party, a man called Ball, slipped away. Again it was pure chance that his absence was noted. Scott played hell.'

'Scott? Michael Scott? What *is* he exactly?'

'He's our sort of trouble-shooter. He keeps an eye on all the colleges. Acts as liaison man with the locals.'

'Do you like him?' asked Emily.

'I don't know,' said Carruthers with a shrug. 'He was, is, a . . . dangerous man, I think. He went after Ball, got to him too late. I don't know what happened exactly, but Ball's body turned up on the sands down near Allonby the next morning.'

'That was one of your men? But I thought it was a foreigner? I thought there was something about his teeth?'

Carruthers nodded.

'We do a thorough job here. If we're caught alive that's tough. But there's no point in letting a dead body do any talking for you. There's lots of ways a corpse can advertise its nationality. We rearrange as many of these as possible. A dentist wouldn't think the National Health ever had anything to do with my mouth!

'Well, with Ball gone, the trail seemed dead. The rest of us were let off the hook. But the heat's still on till at least the fortnight's up. We don't know whether Ball made a contact or not. Certainly he didn't have the tape when Scott

199

reached him. And there's been plenty of activity recently.'

Emily sat on the bed, her head buzzing with the extraordinary story she had just heard.

'Activity?' she said faintly.

'Yes. Castell was killed.'

'Fenimore? What had he to do with it?'

Carruthers raised his eyebrows as though at her naivety.

'The Americans wanted to stake out the area for themselves. Naturally. Conn came here. The Castells were his plant at the hotel. They obviously stirred something up, something, after what happened to you, to do with those two phoney archaeologists. And you yourself were a problem.'

'How?'

'Well, when the wife of the overall head of training suddenly appears on the scene under a false name at a time like this, people start worrying. Mr. Follett has been in touch with the situation from the start. Three days ago he appeared in person.'

'I got the impression he was being put on the spot a little before,' said Emily invitingly.

'In a place like this, at a time like this, everyone's got to be ready to stand up and explain themselves. Everyone.'

'I see,' said Emily thoughtfully. 'What's happening now?'

'We have launched a search for Scott and for Inwit and Plowman. There was no sign of Michael. They found the rowing boat, but there's no trace of the other two.'

200

'Who were they?'

He shrugged. 'Almost certainly working for the opposition. Nasty people from the sound of them.'

'And why me? Why was I involved?'

It was a question she would be expected to ask. But she felt she knew the answer already.

He looked at her curiously.

'I don't know, Mrs. Follett. Perhaps you can tell me?'

Emily sat in silence for a long while, trying to organise her thoughts into some kind of coherence. Carruthers kept very quiet, watching her carefully. There was an air of expectancy in the room.

'I don't know if I can,' said Emily finally. 'There is something . . . Listen, I'd like to talk to my husband if I may. Could you tell him?'

'Certainly, Mrs. Follett. It's been a pleasure talking to you.'

'By the way, Captain,' she asked curiously, 'how does it come that someone of so junior a rank as yourself knows so much about my husband?'

'Rank in an establishment like this is a matter of convenience,' he said with a smile. 'Old Petard's the only one of us who's ever had Her Majesty's commission in a straightforward way. Robin Glover's the real boss here. As for me, I'm just a kind of superior filing clerk!'

He went swiftly from the room, closing the door gently behind him. There was no sound, but when she went to it a moment later it was, as she half expected, locked.

She returned to her seat on the bed and to her still turbulent thoughts. She hadn't yet made up her mind whether the humanity of the green men was a comfort or not.

But for the first time since she had known him Sterne seemed to have put himself in her power. And she had no idea what to do about it.

9

It was more than two hours before anyone came. Curiously she did not mind the wait, though she was not normally a very patient woman. She lay full length on the bed and stared at the ceiling, occasionally nearly drifting into sleep so that the expanse of white plaster turned into the snow slopes in the Harz where Sterne had taken her to learn to ski, or the pale, pale sand which curved like the new moon round the royal blue sea of the Caribbean. Then she would start back to full waking as the memory of Scott, the blood trickling between his fingers, returned to her.

Thinking of Scott made her wonder what had happened to Miranda. She fervently hoped that Inwit had not reached her with his trenching tool. And the thought of Miranda made her sit up violently on the bed as she remembered Cal. Poor Cal! Told to stay on guard at the cottage. What dreadful fears must be lying there with him now, for she was convinced he would not have moved. All his instincts would be telling him to go out and look for her. But the conditioned reflex was of great strength too. The memory of her command would not soon weaken.

She rose now and went to the window and looked out along the shore in the direction of the cottage. But it was out of sight as she knew it would be. She turned her gaze back to the sea, raised it and looked at the American base, so clear in the sunlight it looked like a scale model only a few yards away. Once again she thought of the story Carruthers had told her. She still shivered at the memory of the green men, but she finally decided it was better than ghosts, and ghouls, and green knights. Plowman had sounded curiously expert, but why not? A man does not have to be a moron to be a spy and murderer.

She looked down at the placid sea and wondered if either of the archaeologists had been able to reach the shore. She doubted it. She would have no qualms of conscience if they had not done so. None at all. Conscience was a strange thing, not absolute as the moralists would have you believe, but relative, susceptible to all the pressures of habit, circumstance, loyalty, which affected all decisions and attitudes. It was not the fact that Inwit and Plowman were enemies of her country that cleansed her of guilt in the likelihood of their deaths, but her personal relationship with them, the terror they had caused her and their murder of big, happy, harmless Fenimore Castell.

Harmless? What did she know about that? He had been one of these men too. Plowman himself had seemed jolly in an almost Dickensian way. It was the memory of Amanda, collapsed, faded, destroyed almost, which was affecting her judgment.

So what was she debating about now? Was she trying to persuade herself to action or against it? Was what she thought she knew significant or not? No, that was a stupid evasive question. The answer was obvious.

I suppose it comes down to love, liking, the loyalties of the heart, returning pleasure for pleasure and pain for pain, she thought, half mockingly as she made up her mind.

And turned to find Sterne watching her from the open door.

'May I come in?' he asked.

'Of course,' she said.

'You have had a terrible experience, my dear,' he said, closing the door.

'Do you mean our marriage or last night?' she gibed, feeling it necessary once more to attack.

He did not even look pained.

'All this must have come as a complete surprise to you, my dear. I am sorry for the deception that has been necessary all these years. But it was not so much a deception as a non-sharing, wasn't it? Not the same thing as another woman, for instance.'

There was no question mark in his voice, but he paused as though for a reply.

'If you say so, Sterne,' she said.

He nodded as if satisfied.

'It was, after all, in the service of my, our, country. There was some slight element of risk every time I went behind the Iron Curtain, and I apologise for involving you in this.'

'Thank you,' said Emily. 'What about involving me in *this*?'

She moved her hand to encompass the college, the Grune, the past three days.

'That was an error of judgment,' he said carefully. 'The second I have made concerning you, my dear. The first, of course, was marrying you.'

He smiled sweetly as he uttered the insult. Emily felt a great urge to slap the back of her hand across his mouth, but held herself back. It would keep till later.

'Why me, Sterne?' she asked quietly.

'Marriage or this?' he said, mockingly echoing her own early mockery. 'Not that it isn't the same thing in the end, of course. Strangely enough, I married you for love. Not perhaps what you in your then near-childish naivety would have called love. I found you not unintelligent, physically extremely attractive and above all malleable. You inspired creativity in me, my dear, and that is what I think of as love. I could have had women as beautiful, and much more gifted, sitting as hostess at my table any time I wished. But they would have been bought. Not that I minded that. The straightforward economic relationship is always the best I have found. So clean, so simple. But you invited me into the messy business of creation, and I succumbed.'

'Weak of you,' said Emily, feeling incredulously that in a way he believed he was paying her compliments.

'An indulgence, yes,' he corrected. 'I enjoyed it for a long time. Till I had finished, and you were perfect for the job, or should have been. But creation's a messy business. The suppleness of clay is what makes it the material of the potter. But once moulded and graven and glazed, its suppleness is gone. If you drop it it breaks. And if you're not careful it can cut you.'

'Hurrah for the analogy,' said Emily. 'You talk in metaphors and parables, you and the Bible both. Let's get up to date, shall we?'

'Certainly,' he agreed. 'My second error of judgment, not so serious by half, I'm glad to say, was to ask you to perform this little task for me. It seemed harmless enough, an inspired extemporisation, I felt. It would also have involved you all-unknowing in something that could carry with it a considerable prison sentence. I like everyone connected with me to have some little black mark against their name in the law's book, or rather in my book to be transferred to the law's if necessary. Take young Burgess, for instance. He has had some interesting and spectacular sexual adventures in his time. I could show you pictures which would surprise you. I was touched by the near normality of his interest in you. He had to be reprimanded quite severely a couple of times.'

He was talking freely, far too freely, Emily thought uneasily. He was an accomplished persuader when he wished and could easily have put up some fairly substantial smokescreen. But he didn't seem to care in the least.

'Why are you telling me all this, Sterne?' she heard herself asking. She didn't really want an answer, though what possible answer could bother her she couldn't see.

'Tell me, my dear,' he replied. 'If I had told you that this business at the college had nothing to do with my requesting you to come here, would you have believed me? That it was just coincidence?'

'I don't believe in coincidence,' she said. 'Do you?'

'No. I don't,' said Sterne. She didn't feel her question had been answered, but decided not to press it.

'This tape. Was it going to be in the book?'

'Originally, yes,' he said. 'There were all kinds of changes of plan. In theory the Americans wouldn't have missed a thing till next day, and our people at the college wouldn't have been alerted till the debriefing on return. The book was in the college library, a little cavity ready prepared in the spine for the tape. But things went wrong. Ball had to hide the tape on the Grune — he knew as soon as the Yanks spotted them that they'd all be searched when they got back. He had to be the one to pick it up again. It was so small that only the hider could stand much chance of finding it, especially at night. So off he set to get it. He had the book with him. But Scott spotted he was missing and went in pursuit. Whether he actually got to the tape or not, I do not know. Nor what happened to the book.'

'Which was to have been passed on to me.'

'Eventually. I did not know about these complications when I phoned you. I almost cancelled the arrangement when I heard what had happened, but on second thought it seemed worth while letting it stand. It's always a good thing to have as many strings to your bow as possible.'

He smiled. 'There you are, dear. I am an enemy agent. You protected me downstairs when you did not know for sure, but must have suspected greatly. What are you going to do now the words have been spoken?'

He might have been asking her to dance, the way he stood quietly and confidently before her.

'Sterne,' she replied at last. 'You mean nothing to me. Understand that. In the past I have owed you something, I suppose. Much, by your scale of values, I think. Most of that debt has long since been repaid in a variety of ways. I have suffered, in great comfort I know, but I have suffered none the less. However, I had decided before you came in that if there was any of that debt left in your mind, if I still owed anything at all, now I would finally cancel it out by my silence.'

He nodded approvingly, not so much at her decision, she felt, but at some conclusion of his own.

She went on. 'Then, however, I wasn't absolutely sure. I was merely in possession of information which made you look very suspicious indeed. Things have changed. Now I know for certain. I'm not sure if I can keep quiet now.'

He nodded again, like an approving tutor.

'Good. Good. I'm glad to see how correct my analysis of your thought processes has been. There was a slight risk involved in letting young Carruthers tell you the story. You might have told him about our chat on the telephone that night. But I made a little wager with myself that you wouldn't.'

He allowed himself a slight almost secret smile of self-congratulation.

But he wanted me to be certain of the truth, Emily thought. He didn't want me to keep quiet. Or to be willing to keep quiet. Why?

'And I thought your mind would work exactly along the line you've described, my dear. Well. It may be some little consolation to you to know that I had decided to kill you no matter what conclusion you came to.'

The words did not mean anything at first to Emily. Then she began to laugh as convincingly as she could. It was ludicrous. He must know what a fool he was making of himself. He stared at her intently.

'You know,' he said, 'I feel a strange desire to make love to you for one last time before we part forever. You wouldn't feel able to pander to the whims of an old secret agent, would you?'

Still laughing, she shook her head.

'No,' he said as if to himself. 'I suppose not. A younger man, you're ready for a younger man now. Scott, perhaps, if he were not drowned by now. Or even Burgess.'

'Scott drowned?' she said chokingly, all laughter gone. 'Has he been found?'

'Oh no. Then you are concerned? How touching. No, there's no sign anywhere. Which can only mean the worst. Or the best, perhaps. He was a very dangerous kind of man. I've been trying to edge him out for some little time.

'Well, my love, if you're in no mood for the pleasures of the flesh, perhaps we should make an end of the matter.'

210

Emily suddenly felt a desperate need to play for time.

'Burgess. You mentioned Burgess. What's he got to do with all this?'

'Nothing really. Another creation of mine. I felt it best to have you watched. Also should your real identity be discovered, Burgess was a good support for my role as the jealous husband having his errant wife spied upon. You saw how effective this was earlier. Petard's a shrewd old stick, but too ready to accept the situation he thinks he understands. Have you slept with Burgess, by the way?'

'No!' Emily was surprised at her own indignation.

'Oh. I wondered if his feeling for you could have taken him that far. But he did his job well; within his limitations, that is. Well, I think it's time.'

He looked at his watch.

'I'm lunching with the Lord Lieutenant of the County in forty-five minutes.'

Suddenly terror was reborn in Emily's throat. This was worse than last night. The sun was shining outside, birds singing. Distantly she could see some people playing on the beach by the water's edge. They had a tiny dog with them. She thought of Cal and tears filled her eyes.

'Don't cry,' said Sterne in a kindly voice. She knew then he was mad, and knew that she had known it for years. Not mad in a raving, eccentric, immediately observable way, but quietly, obsessively, terrifyingly mad. An insanity

211

which had given him the strength of will and character to develop power from weakness, riches from poverty, and which then had taken him further and further, till he had become this. She knew why he had betrayed his country. Not for political theory, she was sure of that. Money would help, but not be enough. No, it was a question of taking all the power you had under one system and secretly putting it at the disposal of another system. That way you doubled your power.

All these thoughts mixed confusedly, obscurely, with the vapours of terror which were now clouding her brain. Why she felt so frightened she did not know. He was powerfully built and fit, but he was nearly sixty. He had no weapon, or at least he had not yet produced one. She would certainly leave her mark on him if it came to a struggle. Her screams would be heard. There were other people in the house, perhaps in neighbouring rooms.

And in any case how did he hope to explain either her disappearance, if that could be arranged, or the presence of her obviously assaulted body?

No. She banished that question firmly from her mind. Difficulties of explanation after the event were of no real consolation to her.

She began to move slowly to the door. He obviously noticed, but made no move to stop her. His utter lack of concern was the most frightening thing of all.

She turned the handle. She didn't recollect Sterne using a key after he came in, but nevertheless the door was locked. He nodded as if reading her mind.

'I'm sorry,' he said. 'You'll just have to knock till someone comes.'

It was crazy. Her throat was quite dry with fear. She began to shake the door handle with her left hand and beat on the panel with the other. She realised instantly it was a very very solid door.

'Harder,' he urged, glancing at his watch. 'Harder.'

She obeyed, knowing why she did but not why he'd given the order. Now she began to shout too.

At last, beautifully clear, there was a little click in the lock and the handle turned. She stood back from the door as it opened inwards.

Major Glover stood there, a look of faint concern on his face.

'Thank God!' she said with heartfelt relief and stepped towards him.

He glanced across at Sterne who shook his head. The Major put his hand on her right breast and pushed firmly. She staggered back two steps into the room. He came right in and locked the door behind him.

'Major!' she cried fearfully, still not comprehending what was happening. 'He's a spy! It's him! He's behind it all. Please, let me out! Fetch the Colonel!'

'As you can see, Glover,' said Sterne rather sadly, 'she's bent on talking. I tried to convince her it was all an error, an absurd coincidence, but I couldn't. We'll have to quiet her.'

'A pity,' said the Major. He looked at Emily as if he meant it.

'Oh no,' she said, drawing back against the wall. 'Not you too.'

'Why, Emily!' said Sterne, 'you didn't think I could manage alone?'

She didn't know whether he meant the organisation of the college or her murder. She didn't want to know.

'The orders had to be swapped round,' went on Sterne. 'Everyone blamed poor Ball for that too, but it was really outside his scope.'

'Let's hurry it up, shall we?' said Glover.

Emily was still sufficiently alert to notice the lack of deference in his tone.

'I'm sorry about this,' he said, in a voice full of genuine apology. 'You should have got out after I gave you that scare.'

'Scare?' she said faintly.

'Yes. When I saw you through the window.'

'That was you? The first green man?'

'I'm afraid so. Just checking that Ball hadn't dropped the book in before Scott got to him. You shouldn't have been so brave.'

'She is brave, isn't she?' said Sterne in a tone full of possessive pride. 'Listen, my dear. What we are going to do with you is quite simple. The Major here is one of our most expert 'green men', as you call them. He is going to break your neck with a simple little jerk, then we are going to push you from the window. Or rather the Major is after I've left for my luncheon engagement. I will, of course, testify to your extreme nervous tension, your great excitability. I

214

have enough influence to keep the whole sad business very quiet indeed. Not as quiet as you, of course.'

Emily began to scream. Glover, who had moved quietly behind her as Sterne talked, put his hand over her mouth and pinched her nose with his thumb and finger at the same time.

'Don't gloat,' he said to Sterne in a voice full of disgust.

Emily felt a sharp pricking sensation at the base of her spine. For a second she thought this was some fearful prelude to the cracking of her neck, but Glover released her gently on to the bed and she saw the hypodermic in his hand.

'What did you do that for?' demanded Sterne. 'They'll spot the puncture.'

'Unlikely,' said the Major. 'It's better to have her quiet when it's done. There mustn't be any sign of a struggle.'

Emily felt a terrible weakness begin to drift through her body.

'Look,' said Glover. 'Isn't there some other way? Do we have to . . . ?'

'I wasn't going to tell,' said Emily faintly. 'He's doing this for himself, his own satisfaction!'

'Is she right?' asked the Major, eyeing Sterne sharply.

'She is a dying woman. She would say anything to save herself,' said Sterne coldly. Suddenly he seemed to have lost all interest. 'As you've managed to put her in that state, you can finish the job quite easily by yourself. I really must go or I'll be very late. Of course, I shan't get any lunch when I get there. The news of my wife's death will be waiting for me, and I'll have to come straight back. What a charade it all is!'

He unlocked the door and turned the handle. Glover turned to Emily, pity in his eyes.

He's looking at me like a pet that's to be put down. The sooner it's done, the better! thought Emily in panic. Her strength had almost entirely gone.

Then the door burst open violently, catching Sterne full in the chest and flinging him back into the room so that he fell on the bed across her legs.

Standing in the doorway, his dark face haggard and unshaven, his left shoulder bandaged round and round and his arm in a sling was Michael Scott. In his other hand was a big, beautiful gun.

He took a step forward and kicked the door shut behind him so that he could see the entire room.

'Emily,' he said. 'Are you all right?'

Tears began to stream down her face. She was absurdly, ludicrously touched that his first words were addressed to her.

Sterne lay still on the bed. She knew he wouldn't move till he saw reason for it. But she saw something else very curious through her tears. Michael was paying no attention at all to Glover. It crossed her mind that he considered Glover no threat. And she could see the same realisation dawning on the Major's face.

'Michael,' she tried to cry warningly. 'Michael.' But the words came out pathetically, brokenly, and with a snarl of anger he pushed Sterne off the bed on to the floor and bent over her.

He must have seen something of what she meant in her eyes, however, for the look of tenderness on his face changed and he swung round to see Glover's fist descending on him.

He was quick enough to fall away under the blow, but he couldn't evade the foot that snaked rapidly out and hacked the automatic from his grasp.

He scrambled to his feet and for a moment the two men crouched facing each other.

'This *is* a surprise, Robin,' said Scott softly.

'That's a real compliment coming from you,' grinned Glover, and threw himself at his opponent. There was no room to sidestep, and Michael was carried back to smash against the wall. Emily saw him twist at the last moment so that it was his good shoulder which hit first. Even then the pain the sudden jar must have cost him was evident in the twisting of his face as he grappled one-armed with the Major.

Glover's expertise as a 'green man' was obvious to the most inexpert eye. With Michael fit it would have been a desperately even contest. But now as they got back to their feet again, as though by mutual agreement, he was able to come rushing in chopping with both hands while Scott could merely use his good arm to ward off some of the blows. His only counters came with the feet and these Glover evaded with contemptuous ease. The whole bout would have been finished in under a minute if Sterne hadn't taken a hand.

He rose to a kneeling position by the side of the bed.

The movement caught Emily's eye.

He's saying his prayers! was her first frivolous reaction. Then she saw Michael's automatic in his hands. He held it out before him and took aim two-handed. Michael was finished now, hardly able to stand up, leaning back against the door.

Glover looked across at Sterne and made a gesture of negation at the gun which Sterne ignored. His fingers pulled back the trigger.

Emily with a monumental effort rolled sideways and fell out of the bed on top of him.

There were three sharp explosions in rapid succession. A red-hot cartridge was ejected on to her dress and she could smell the fabric smouldering. She rolled over again so that it was dislodged, and raised her head.

Michael stood alone by the door, looking down. Where Glover had been standing there were three crimson-stained irradiations of plaster in the wall. They were smudged downwards to where the Major sat slumped forward on the floor. He was obviously dead.

Sterne rose beneath her, unceremoniously thrusting her aside. He still had the gun in his hand. He looked down unemotionally at Glover.

'Providence is a mysterious force,' he said. 'You look in bad shape, Scott.'

'I'll do,' said Michael sourly.

'If I let you,' said Sterne.

He stood in thought for a moment, the gun levelled unwaveringly at Michael's chest.

'We couldn't come to some arrangement, I suppose?' he said.

'No.'

Silence again.

'There'll be others coming now, I take it?'

'Certainly.'

He nodded, came to a decision.

'Here, then. It's better you should have this.'

He reversed the gun in his hand, blew on his fingers as they encountered the hot barrel, and handed it over to Scott.

'I've no desire to end like *that*,' he said with distaste, indicating Glover's body. 'Why go in for heroics? I'll get thirty years, I daresay, but with what I know, I'll be out in two or three. A couple of business men. A student perhaps. They'll pick them up till they've got enough for a nice package deal. Why, with the information I've given them, they could go out tomorrow and bring in a dozen.'

He's nervous, thought Emily. That's turned him garrulous. But it's probably true.

Looking at Scott, she saw he thought so too. His face went even tauter, if that were possible, and she thought for a moment he was going to press the trigger. Resisting arrest. She'd have gladly lied for him.

But he glanced at her and relaxed. She knew it was just her presence that had saved Sterne.

He seemed to sense this too and bent over her, his old courtesy returning like a parody of itself.

'Let me give you a hand, my dear,' he said, drawing her up to her knees.

'Come on!' said Scott, savagely opening the door.

It must have looked as if Sterne had knocked her down, said Emily later, defensively. But privately she believed it would have made no difference at all.

Through the open door she heard the sound of footsteps. Many footsteps, running fast. The shots must have been heard. However dulled, however distant, shots were things the men in this house would recognise instantly.

That was what she heard. But what she saw in the doorway was not a man. It was an avenging demon, a brown and white fury, huge with red mouth wide agape and white teeth shining horribly beneath the tightly drawnback lips.

'Cal!' she shouted.

He cleared the gap between them in a single bound, propelled clear off the ground by the thrust of his powerful haunches. No sound came from him. His outstretched front legs caught Sterne Follett full in the chest. He was thrust back against the wall, all poise, elegance, control, authority gone.

He had time for a single cry.

'Emily!' he screamed.

Then the great dog took him by the throat and severed veins, arteries, windpipe and all with a single constriction of his jaws.

He didn't worry the body, but turned immediately from the lifeless husk before it had even slid down to the floor. Now he barked once joyfully at Emily, who put her arm defensively round his neck and held herself between him and the group of dumbstruck men who stood in horror by the door.

'He put his eye out,' she sobbed. 'It was Sterne that blinded him. It was Sterne.'

Then her voice became inaudible in her weeping.

10

'Sterne could not bear imperfection,' she said quietly. 'Everything had to be flawless. That's how I got in on the act in the first place. That sounds vain, I know, but physically I was dead lucky. Skin, hair, eyes, proportions; at eighteen I was in peak condition.'

'You're like something in a remnant sale now,' said Michael Scott, examining her critically. Her nose was still invisible beneath its dressing, her arms and legs crisscrossed with scratches from gorse and briar.

'Snap,' she said. He laughed and moved his arm in its sling to show how trivial it all was. She saw him wince.

'It serves you right for showing off,' she said. 'Glover made a good job of your face too.'

He said nothing, but she felt his eyes fixed on her behind the bruise-concealing dark glasses.

'Anyway,' she said, 'when Cal was born I was lucky enough to see him first. Sterne loved thoroughbreds, or rather admired them, gave them his lordly approval. If he had seen Cal before I did, the poor beast would have been destroyed on the spot.'

She laughed at the memory of her first acquaintance with the puppy.

'Mind you, he did look odd. I can't imagine what his mother had been up to.'

'Can't you?'

She ignored him.

'So I helped myself to him, brought him up secretly for several weeks, but he soon grew too large for concealment. When Sterne saw him he told me to get rid of him. I refused. This was the first time I'd ever really stood up to him, I think. But I needed Cal even more than he needed me at that time. Sterne shrugged, told me to keep him out of his way and that seemed to be that. Cal grew and grew and grew. Naturally he became interested in finding himself a bitch. There wasn't much future in the average mongrel running loose in the park, not at his size. So with great ingenuity he sought out and began to court two or three of the thoroughbred Danes Sterne bred on his estate.'

She went silent. They were standing on the shore almost at the Point watching the waters run swiftly down the estuary. It was the second day after Sterne had died.

'And?' Scott prompted gently. She had to finish what she had started.

'Sterne found him there. He had a heavy brass-embossed riding crop with him. He beat him round the head with it, driving him back out of the pen. Cal didn't have enough sense to run, and he was too gentle to attack.'

'He's changed.'

'Just for Sterne. He never forgot. When the vet cleared up the mess and dressed the wounds, he told me that he was blind in one eye. After that, just the smell of Sterne round the house, the sound of his footstep two rooms away, set his anger going. I think it was that also that finally made up my mind for me. It took another three months but I did it. I left Sterne.'

Silence again. A seagull floated low over them, cruciform in flight, its wings laid back stiffly from the beautifully barrelled aerodynamic body. Like a trout with wings.

'Would you have brought Cal with you if you'd known?' Emily asked suddenly.

'What he would do to Sterne? I don't know. I really had no choice. When I crawled into your cottage that night he made me very welcome. He even extended his courtesy to Miranda when she turned up an hour later. She always finds me out in the end, like a real woman. They wanted to lick me better between them. But I managed to ring the doctor nevertheless, just for a second opinion. Rogers knows something of the college. He has to. We have injuries on exercises, that kind of thing, which are to say the least suspicious. So when he saw the state I was in he kept it quiet, gave me a jab and put me to bed in the cottage. When I woke up it was light. I got in touch with Parfrey. He told me you were all right.'

'Parfrey!'

'Very bright lad, is Parfrey. All kinds of special duties. You'd be surprised how many extra-intelligent local constables there are near Government establishments like this. He'd been out investigating reports of a capsized rowing boat, floating down the Firth. Something to do with you, I presume?'

He looked questioningly at her. She didn't reply, so he went on.

'He met some of our chaps out searching for me and heard they'd picked you up. I was very relieved for a while.'

'Just for a while.'

'Yes,' said Scott, eyeing her steadily. 'Then I found some very interesting bedside reading, and I began to wonder.'

'What do you mean?'

From inside his jacket slung loosely over his shoulders because of the sling he produced a squat dumpy book which Emily recognised at once.

'Why, that's my history of the Solway!' she said.

'Yours?' he questioned.

'Well, it belongs to the cottage.'

Silently he opened the back cover and held it out to her. There in a circular purple stamp, faded but clearly legible, she read 'Property of Skinburness Teachers' Training College.'

'You mean this is *the* book?' she asked incredulously.

He turned it over, inserted his thumb into a cut in the spine and pulled down sharply. The leather peeled back like a banana skin. Carefully he extracted what looked like a strip of celluloid about one-eighth by one-third of an inch.

'Is that the tape?'

He nodded.

'Well, isn't it . . . shouldn't you *do* something before it's too late? I thought there was a time limit?'

'Oh no,' he laughed. 'This stuff lasts forever.'

So saying he crushed it between his finger and

225

thumb and flicked it out to sea.

'All right,' said Emily. 'You've impressed me with your medieval Michael Scot act. Now explain.'

'It's simple,' he said. 'We'd been on to Ball for some time. As soon as the Americans rang us up that night, I headed down to the landing spot, tracked Ball back, picked up the tape from the middle of the briar patch where he'd put it under a stone, and returned later to substitute a piece of my own. We had to arrest them all on arrival back at the college, it would have looked very odd if we hadn't after they'd aroused the Yanks' guards. But we gave Ball plenty of room. And spread around this story about the stuff's decayability. Ball took me by surprise, I must admit. Looking back, I can see Robin Glover must have had a hand in it. In fact, I was having a drink with Glover when the news came that he was missing. I went out after him. I was pretty sure he had dropped the tape by the time I got him in my sights. But I let him keep running just in case. Then he just went out like a light in the water. It was his heart. We were fools. If we'd checked back we'd have found his medical report had been altered to get him on the training course. And while a man's security background can be built up over a great number of years, a medical report could only be fiddled recently, by someone at the top. Follett must have been getting delusions of grandeur to take such a risk.'

'It seems absurd that he got himself personally involved in the business in any case,' said Emily, stooping to pick a piece of sea-holly, then changing her mind as a sense of its beauty reached her. Its fragile thistle-flower and the delicate pastel green of its leaves made the shiny vulgarity of Christmas holly seem like a plastic imitation, she thought.

'Yes, it does. His controllers won't be pleased. He was in an ideal position. Men like Ball and Glover were meant as sleepers, I imagine. People who would flourish and progress in British security till they reached their peak. *Then* begin to work. But Sterne blew these two and himself. He learnt about the tape somehow — he had that kind of connection — and must have thought he'd impress everyone by getting it. I'm certain he wasn't given instructions. It wouldn't have been worth it.'

'Why? What was on the tape?'

The wind flattened her dress against her body, pushing a fold of cloth between her legs. She knew the effect was dramatic, watched Scott surreptitiously to see if he noticed. He didn't appear to, but the dark glasses hid a lot.

'Just some figures. Information about U.S. nuclear submarine positions in the next month. Useful only if you want to start a war, which we don't think anyone does at the moment.'

'I'm glad,' she said, turning her back into the wind to give her rear silhouette a chance. 'You were saying about the tape. You thought Ball had delivered it somewhere. So what did you in your wisdom decide to do?'

'Nothing. We kept the options wide open to encourage interest. It worked. Inwit and

Plowman turned up out of nowhere and began excavating non-existent medieval sites in the middle of gorse bushes. Glover must have got some vague idea of the hiding-place from Ball, and it wasn't certain that he'd even managed to pick the tapes up. Then you appear, though we'd no idea who you were for some days. Follett was very clever there sending Burgess after you so he could let himself be the one to reveal who you were and so cover himself with the jealous-husband story. And then Follett himself comes to make a personal check on everything, as he put it.'

'Did you suspect Sterne, then?'

'Everybody who works in Security is suspected,' he said slowly. 'Me included. The only person I really trusted at the college was Robin Glover, I think, which just goes to show. No; Follett was probably less suspect than anyone else, because he wasn't on the spot. In any case, Ball might have been absolutely alone as far as the college went. We were just interested in seeing where the trail led. We decided to let Inwit and Plowman find the tape. Fenimore Castell had got in with them without rousing their suspicions he thought. He knew where their next dig was proposed and went out that night to plant another false tape. They must have been on to him. Plowman told Mrs. Castell her husband was still alive and would remain so as long as she played ball. We put our nurse in to keep an eye on her. She looked about ready to spill everything to those two.'

Emily felt slightly faint. Even the cool breeze

off the water didn't seem refreshing.

'It's a strange business,' she said. 'Nothing is certain.'

'You cover as many chances as you can. That's all,' said Scott. 'Like you. You were just another chance as far as Follett was concerned. When you didn't come back to London, it meant you hadn't received the book. But he still sent Burgess into the cottage to check on you, and Glover to check on Burgess.'

'But why didn't they spot it?'

Scott shrugged. 'Burgess because he didn't really know what he was looking for. A packet of some kind. Not a book on a bedside table. He'd no idea what was going on, of course.'

'Poor Arthur. He'll be out of a job now.'

'We might find him something. He seems to have a talent for snooping.'

There was a little scorn in his voice.

'Miaow,' said Emily. 'Remember pots and kettles. What about Glover?'

'He never got as far as your bedroom, did he? Which was where the book was. They both had keys to the cottage, of course, kindly supplied by your husband.'

'I wondered how he got me into the cottage after I was attacked. My keys were in the lane.'

She shivered. 'At least they didn't harm me.'

'No. But don't forget that Inwit and Plowman were working for him as well. Inwit extemporised when he saw you pick up my notebook. It might have been the one. Burgess thought that too. He picked it up in the lane and pocketed it. We found it in Follett's room. Burgess must have been invited to deliver it the next day.'

'Yes. Yes,' said Emily slowly. 'I worked that out.'

'But to get back to my first point, I'm certain Follett gave those two ghouls *carte blanche* as far as you were concerned. It would have been easier than a divorce if you'd been found floating in the Solway.'

'I nearly was,' said Emily.

They had walked all the way round the Point as they talked, down along the creek, so engrossed in their conversation that neither had noticed the row-boat which Inwit and Plowman had taken was returned to its berth. Now they were passing alongside the hotel. A taxi had drawn up outside and two people were getting into it, obviously sharing it to the nearest station. Cases were being stacked in the boot.

They were Burgess and Mrs. Castell.

Amanda saw them and came across. She looked better now, but still haggard, still feeling sorrow deep, deep inside.

'Goodbye, honey,' she said to Emily. 'And thanks. You too, Mr. Scott. They got the tape back, I guess?'

'Yes, Mrs. Castell,' said Scott gently. 'They got it back.'

'Well, that's something, I suppose. See you, hon.'

She turned back to the taxi.

'Doesn't she *know*?' whispered Emily fiercely.

'That we had the tape all the time? No. Do *you* want to tell her?'

Burgess held the door open for the old

woman. He looked uneasily across at Scott and Emily, obviously uncertain whether to speak or not.

'Goodbye, Arthur,' said Emily firmly.

He turned without answering and climbed into the cab. He didn't look out of the window as it drove away.

'I think he fancied you,' said Scott casually.

'Yes. I think he did,' she answered, just as casually. 'I might have fancied him at first. You know, one of the first things he told me was that people often said he was like an echo. He had this habit of repeating what you said. But to me he would always be a different kind of echo. An echo of Sterne.'

They began to walk down the lane to the cottage.

'You never told me what you did when you found the book in my bedroom.'

'Well, of course I knew instinctively what the explanation was. Ball had dropped it in a great hurry, realising I was close behind. No time to wrap it up or write a covering note. He probably lobbed it through a window, or something.'

'Why, yes. I found it lying open on the bed, I remember.'

'Yes, I thought it must have been something like that. Some perfectly innocent explanation.'

'So what did you do?'

'I searched the cottage from top to bottom, of course. What else?'

'Why, you bastard!'

She swung her fist threateningly at his injured shoulder, but his other hand came up and caught it in a vice-like grip.

'I found a fascinating selection of kinky lingerie,' he went on. 'I also found a letter you'd written to your husband, telling him you were backing out of the deal. That told me all I wanted to know. I set off post haste to the college. And Cal made it quite clear he was coming with me.'

She released herself from him gently.

'I'm glad in a way he did.'

'So am I. Follett was right. He'd caused death, disaster, tragedy to God knows how many people. Not just here, but everywhere he'd been in a position of trust. And he'd have probably been exchanged in a matter of years, or less.'

'What made him do it, Michael?'

'Power,' he replied. 'A sense of his own supremacy. I don't know. He was a great organiser, there's no doubt. God knows how many of their men he's inched into positions of responsibility in our European units and through the training colleges. We'll have to back-check everyone's file to see if there's a point where Follett's word or decision alone let him in. Not that that proves anything either. It's a mess.'

They were nearly at the cottage now.

'Never mind,' she said, trying to lift the blackness which had descended on to his face. 'A touch of the old Scott magic will turn everything to gold. Then you'll only have a golden mess.'

'Christ. Look at that!' he said, ignoring her frivolity.

They were at the cottage gate. Lying across the threshold, head uplifted to acknowledge their arrival, was Cal. His great forelegs were splayed open in front of him. Between them, her head resting on one gigantic paw, was Miranda. She rolled on her back, exposing her belly to the sky in pleasure at their approach. Cal bent forward, nudged her into a more decorous position, and licked her affectionately with his great red tongue.

'Cal, of course, is short for Caliban?' Michael said suddenly.

'Yes, it is.'

'That's a turn-up for the book,' he said. 'The monster getting the girl.'

'They do say that animals grow like their owners,' said Emily coyly.

'Aren't things the wrong way round?' asked Scott, looking down at the great dog which was nuzzling happily at Miranda's belly.

'All the greatest discoveries have been made by adventurous experiment,' said Emily.

'In that case,' said Scott, 'perhaps you'd care to carry me over the threshold.'

Laughing together, arm in arm, they stepped carefully over the two animals and passed inside. Scott's good arm went round her waist, and his face came down into her hair as she turned to close the door. Desperately trying not to reveal the weakness in her legs, the ball of warm pleasure collecting in her stomach, she paused a moment and looked out towards the Point.

'Tell me,' she said casually, 'who was the second green man, the one who interfered between me and Inwit?'

'I don't know,' he said, uninterested, his voice

muffled by her hair, his lips doing beautiful things to her neck. 'Glover perhaps. We can't ask him. Close the door or you'll have us both in gaol.'

Obediently she pushed the door to and turned gladly towards him. She had a feeling that having his arm in a sling wasn't going to interfere in the slightest with his actions in the immediate future. Besides, he would have every possible help.

Outside over the briar and the tall feathered grass of the Grune, a breeze seemed to run for a moment, gathering speed as it raced to the Point.

Then all was still.

THE END

We do hope that you have enjoyed reading this large print book.

Did you know that all of our titles are available for purchase?

We publish a wide range of high quality large print books including:
Romances, Mysteries, Classics
General Fiction
Non Fiction and Westerns

Special interest titles available in large print are:
The Little Oxford Dictionary
Music Book
Song Book
Hymn Book
Service Book

Also available from us courtesy of Oxford University Press:
Young Readers' Dictionary
(large print edition)
Young Readers' Thesaurus
(large print edition)

For further information or a free brochure, please contact us at:
Ulverscroft Large Print Books Ltd.,
The Green, Bradgate Road, Anstey,
Leicester, LE7 7FU, England.
Tel: (00 44) 0116 236 4325
Fax: (00 44) 0116 234 0205

Other titles in the
Charnwood Library Series:

EATERS OF THE DEAD

Michael Crichton

In A.D. 922 Ibn Fadlan, the representative of the ruler of Bagdad, City of Peace, crosses the Caspian Sea and journeys up the valley of the Volga on a mission to the King of Saqaliba. Before he arrives, he meets with Buliwyf, a powerful Viking chieftain who is summoned by his besieged relatives to the North. Buliwyf must return to Scandinavia and save his countrymen and family from the monsters of the mist . . .

THE SAVAGE SKY

Emma Drummond

1941: Rob Stallard, the unworldly son of a farmer, leaves war-torn London for a Florida airbase along with a group of RAF pilot cadets. He quickly develops a great passion and talent for flying, but is not so happy when he encounters US cadet James Theodore Benson III, son of a senator. Rob is instantly averse to a man who appears to regard flying as merely another string to his sporting bow. For his part, Jim sees Rob as a 'cowpoke from Hicksville'. Personal dislike rapidly extends to professional rivalry, and a near-fatal flying incident creates bitter enmity between them that will last more than a decade.

THE UGLY SISTER

Winston Graham

The Napoleonic Wars have ended as Emma Spry tells her fascinating story . . . One side of her face marred at birth, Emma grows up without affection, her elegant mother on the stage, her father killed in a duel before she was born. Her beautiful sister, Tamsin, is four years the elder, and her mother's ambitions lie in Tamsin's future, and in her own success. A shadow over their childhood is the ominous butler, Slade. Then there is predatory Bram Fox, with his dazzling smile; Charles Lane, a young engineer; and Canon Robartes, relishing rebellion in the young Emma, her wit, her vulnerability, encouraging her natural gift for song.

NOW AND THEN

Joseph Heller

Here is the writer Joseph Heller's Coney Island childhood, down the block from the world's most famous amusement park. It was the height of the Depression, it was a fatherless family, yet little Joey Heller had a terrific time — on the boardwalk, in the ocean, even in school. Then, a series of jobs, from delivering telegrams to working in a Navy yard — until Pearl Harbor, the Air Force, Italy. And after the war, college, teaching, Madison Avenue, marriage, and — always — writing. And finally the spectacular success of CATCH-22, launching one of the great literary careers.

NIGHT PASSAGE

Robert B. Parker

When a busted marriage kicks his drinking problem into overdrive and the Los Angeles Police Department unceremoniously dumps him, Jesse Stone's future looks bleak. So he's shocked when a small Massachusetts town called Paradise recruits him as a police chief. Jesse doesn't have to look for trouble in Paradise: it comes to him. For what is on the surface a quiet New England community quickly proves to be a crucible of political and moral corruption replete with triple homicide, tight Boston mob ties, flamboyantly errant spouses, maddened militiamen, and a psychopath-about-town who has fixed his sights on the new lawman.